For my husband, Jason, whose support and love has never wavered, and for my son, Noah, who inducted me into the world of boy.

chapter 1

CA-CHUNK, CA-CHUNK, CA-CHUNK.

The sound drifts through my bedroom window. Pokes through my homework haze. It's not loud, but it's impossible to ignore. Because it doesn't belong here.

Ca-chunk, ca-chunk, ca-chunk.

Candor sounds the same every night. Hissing sprinklers. Screeching swamp frogs. The drone of the mosquito truck, circling every block.

This doesn't fit.

Ca-chunk, ca-chunk, ca-chunk.

It's getting louder now. I roll back my chair and stand up. There's time for a quick expedition outside. Homework can wait for five minutes. Or more, if this is something interesting.

But one of Dad's Messages streams into my brain. *Academics are the key to success.* Makes my knees lock and my feet weigh a hundred pounds. I'm not going anywhere.

There's homework to do.

The Messages stay filed away until you're about to do something interesting. Your brain knows what to feed you: a Message rushes into your head. Covers everything else. No desire. No fear.

No hunger, even. I sit again and open my bio book.

Another one flows in. *Studying is your top priority.*

"Got it," I say out loud, like my brain is a separate person. "You can shut up now."

Other people don't notice when a Message fills their head. But I've been here longer than anyone. And I've found ways to train myself. I know when my brain is feeding me Messages. I know how to fight them.

When it's worth it.

But tonight there is homework to do. A lot of homework. I stare at my book. Krebs Citric Acid Cycle. Anyone who memorizes it gets fifteen bonus points on the midterm. That should make my score 115. I excel at bio. Like everything.

Ca-chunk, ca-chunk, ca-chunk.

I trace my finger over the cycle diagram. "Isocitrate goes to oxalosuccinate." The words roll around the surface of my brain.

Now I hear a new sound. *Rattle-rattle-rattle.* It's familiar. But what is it?

It wouldn't hurt to take a peek. I flick up one of the wood blind slats above my desk.

I see a row of houses lined up five feet from the sidewalk, each with cozy-lit porches and lush flowerbeds. The broad sidewalk is lined with white picket fences. Plastic fences—they never need painting or termite treatments. Everybody is inside, where they're supposed to be.

Except the girl on the sidewalk. She's bent over. Her arms are bare. Long hair spills over her shoulders and shines in the porch lights.

It's Thursday night. Nobody is supposed to be out. It's time for flash cards, and extra credit, and college essays if there's time. Nobody would *want* to be out. The Messages make sure of that.

Maybe she's new. Maybe she's a potential client for me.

It's been boring lately. I haven't had a playmate in months—fewer people are moving in, and the ones who come lack funds. It's hard to fight being perfect 24/7. I need a release, even if it's something small.

Most of my clients come to Candor with goodies. I make sure they share with me. But right now all I've got is Sherman. He's loaded with the green stuff, but tiresome. He didn't even bring a single dirty magazine when his family moved here.

Sure, I have a girlfriend. But she's so buttoned up, I only keep her as a part of my disguise.

I'm the model Candor boy—a son to brag about. Proof that the Messages work. That's what everyone thinks. Even my dad.

He doesn't know it's all an act. That I've built my own business, a business that makes his customers very unhappy. It's strictly boutique, for a select few. Not many can afford me.

Maybe this girl will.

Never waste our natural resources. I pull the chain on my desk light. Sometimes it's not worth fighting.

More Messages try to push in. They tell me to stay. Study. Avoid distractions. I close my eyes and imagine a wall in my brain. It's made of steel. No cracks for the Messages to seep in.

It's just one of the ways I fight, and it took years to get good at.

Tonight it works. My head is almost silent. But there are thuds behind the wall. Eventually something will break through.

She's standing up when I get outside. Tall, with plenty of curves to stare at.

"Who are you?" I blurt out.

Stupid. I sound like an idiot. Totally out of control.

A one-sided smile lights up her face, but it's gone fast. "Nobody you should care about."

I stare down at her feet. Scuffed combat boots. Rolled-up camis. And a skateboard under one foot.

Ca-chunk, ca-chunk. The sound of a skateboard crossing the sidewalk cracks. Something you never hear in Candor.

Dad hates skateboards—says they're dangerous and destructive. My brother, Winston, used to ride one—before he died being stupid. The Messages make sure everybody else's kids are careful. Kids toss their boards right after they move in.

"You must be new," I say.

"Let's see." She pastes a fake-looking smile on her face. Her voice is overly enthusiastic. "We moved in on Friday. From Boston. No, I don't love it here. No, I don't want to join the debate team or service club or any other little group you're a part of. And I could care less what you got on your SATs."

She's the opposite of nice. But I like hearing someone say what she really thinks.

"You think you're too good for the rest of us?" I say.

She snaps open her mouth and locks her green eyes onto mine. But then she shrugs and looks away. "Never hold yourself above others," she mutters.

That's a Message. Not surprising, if she's been here six days. What's amazing is that she's still mostly *not* Candor.

Not that she'll make it past two weeks. Nobody does.

Not unless I get them out. That's my business. I get new kids out of Candor before they've changed. Back to the real world. It's not cheap, but it's the best deal of their lives.

I wonder if she's got easy access to cash. I also wonder if she's wearing a bra.

"You rich?" I ask. With her, I don't have to bother with Candor fakeness.

"We've got enough." She looks past me, down the sidewalk. Restless.

"Come inside. We have lemonade," I say.

"I hate lemonade."

"We have water. And coffee. Really expensive coffee." My father's only vice.

"Not thirsty." She plants one foot in the middle of her board.

"Whatever. I have to go anyway. I've got bio. And French. And, of course, civics." Stupid mouth. Why won't you stop talking? I sound like I care if she goes. Which I don't. Not much. It's not like I need her money. There's plenty tucked away.

Then I spot something in her hand. A cylinder, shiny, with an orange cap. "Is that spray paint?"

She gives me big eyes, like she's never seen it before. "How'd that get there?"

"You stole it, didn't you?" Thieves are excellent clients. Plenty of cash and toys, and they're always useful on the outside. My clients owe me for life. And I collect.

"I didn't steal it. I . . . bought it."

"Liar. Nobody sells spray paint in Candor."

"Fine. I found it on a construction site. It's half gone anyway." She lifts it and gives it a shake. *Rattle-rattle-rattle.*

The other mystery sound.

"Let me watch." She seems like the graffiti type—not that I've ever seen one before.

Candor is a graffiti-virgin town.

This could be a historic moment.

"Why do you want to watch? Does Daddy need a full report?" She laughs. Its girly, light sound doesn't fit with the combat goth-teen look.

"Do you even know who my father is?"

Those green eyes sweep over me and away.

"Sure. And I know who *you* are. The famous Oscar Banks." She spreads her arms wide, like an announcer on a stage. "Tall, tidy, and handsome. Debate-team captain. Valedictorian. Future savior of the free world."

She thinks I'm handsome. I knew this girl was smart.

"You want an autograph?" I shoot her my best just-kidding smile, but she's not looking. "What's your name, anyway?"

"Like I said, don't waste your time." Her lips twist like she's tasted something sour.

That's fine. I can look her up in Dad's files and get the scoop on whatever she did to land here. Look at her family's credit report.

Right now, I want entertainment. "Let's go paint something." But a Message flows into my brain. *Keep Candor beautiful.* It knows what I want to do and pushes my feet backward, toward the house.

"Not now," I say. Then I shake my head. "Not you," I tell her.

"Get lost, crazy boy."

I fight the Message. Build my wall. I want to be near someone who isn't perfect, doing something she isn't supposed to do.

"If you ditch me, I'll tell my dad," I say. "And he'll tell your parents."

It makes me sound like I'm six, but it'll work on any kid who's lived here a few days.

"So what?" She moves like she's going to roll away, like she doesn't care about getting in trouble. Like she's different from all the other kids here.

But then her leg drops back to the pavement. She sighs. "Always strive to make your parents proud."

Nobody escapes the Messages.

Not that kids understand what's happening. Dad warns their parents never to tell. Children don't understand, he says. They'll get angry. Resistant. It could take longer for the Messages to soak in. It's not like the adults, who can't wait for the Messages to make them — and their less-than-perfect children — new and improved.

I guess he has a point. I found out and I've been fighting them ever since.

She rolls a little closer. "Please don't tell."

"I won't if you let me come."

She snorts. "Like you'd do anything bad. You're just like the rest of them. You're the *king* of the rest of them."

My facade fools her, just like everyone else. That should make me proud. Instead a flush crawls over the back of my neck. I want to prove her wrong.

Our eyes meet. There's something, just for a second. Something that makes her smile. Something that makes my stomach flip.

I reach across her body. Our chests touch for a second. And then I've got the paint can.

I sprint down the sidewalk. I'm not sure where I'm going, except that it's away. Away from my father and the Krebs cycle and being the perfect Oscar Banks.

Just in case someone looks outside, I jam the can under my shirt. Always be ready for just in case.

She's on her board now, rolling next to me. "Give it back," she says.

"No way." I pat the hard metal under my shirt. "It wants to be free."

The Messages are crowding into my brain, trying to correct me before I'm a bad boy. *Vandalism is wrong. Never deface someone else's property.*

Just because I hear them doesn't mean I have to obey. That's what makes me different from the others.

I don't know if I'll win this time. If I'll get to do something I want and the Messages don't. But I'm going to try.

There's a streetlight out on the corner of Persimmon and Longview. Unusual. The street crew will have it fixed before dusk tomorrow—or sooner. A guy with a lightbulb and unquestioning obedience to my father could show up any second.

This will have to be fast. I whip out the paint.

The girl grinds her skateboard to a stop.

"Don't waste it." Her voice is loud. "I need that."

"It's mine now." I uncap the paint and survey my options. The streetlight post? A slick section of fence? The grass?

I press down the button and there's a hissing sound. I'm doing it—making a big orange streak on the post, defacing property. Breaking rules.

My mouth splits into a huge grin. I can taste the tang of the paint.

But the Messages scream in my brain. *Badbadbad.*

I stuff them back. Swing the can wide.

It feels good.

chapter 2

THE NEW MESSAGE is waiting when I walk into school the next morning. That's very bad news for me.

Music is playing from the round white speakers in the ceilings, as always. Today's classical piano. The teachers say the music helps us concentrate, but it's chockful-o'-Messages.

Today the music has a new one.

Tell someone if you know who painted the graffiti.

It floats on top of all my thoughts, bobbing, reminding, not going away. My feet want to take me to the nearest teacher. My mouth wants to spill out the truth. "I did it," I'd say.

But I won't. If Dad found out, he'd send me to the Listening Room, where they take the hard cases and wipe their brains clear. Fill them with nutritious delicious Messages. All my years of fighting would be for nothing.

I picture the steel wall in my brain sliding down like a garage door. The Message is trapped. It can't get me. I can barely hear it behind all that metal.

The quiet in my brain gives me space to think. I realize I have to find the skateboarding girl—now, before she obeys the new Message.

But my girlfriend finds me first.

"Did you hear the news?" Mandi's blue eyes are open wide. She's holding a clipboard. "There's graffiti everywhere."

A tall girl turns the corner ahead of us. Swingy ponytail, pink cardigan, white sneakers. No, definitely not her.

It's a quarter to seven, fifteen minutes before first period. Soon skateboarding girl will be locked behind one door and me behind another. She'll have forty-five minutes for that Message to sink in.

The halls are full of kids putting their backpacks in lockers with no locks. No worries about theft or secrets here. Kids talk, but it's quiet, like the boring cocktail parties my parents used to have in Chicago. It smells like oranges—tile cleaner—and whole-grain waffles. *Healthy breakfasts make for smart minds.*

"Oscar Banks, my man." A short boy wearing a button-down and leather loafers—white socks—claps me on the shoulder. "Care to join us for chess club after school?"

I have never seen this kid in my life.

Or maybe I've seen fifty of them, and they all blend together.

Mandi lets out a loud sigh and taps her clipboard with her pen. She thinks she owns me, which is better than chess boy owning me, at least.

"Gosh darn, I have to study. I sure wish I could make it."

Nobody's an outcast here. The Messages make sure of that. So there are still cliques—like the science nerds, the super studiers, the nutrition freaks—but they all recruit like they get a prize every time a new person sits at their lunch table.

They all want me. I only say yes to an invite when my reputation needs feeding—just enough to keep the Oscar Banks persona alive.

No need to say yes today.

"Chess makes your brain more agile." He taps his head and

raises his eyebrows like we're sharing a secret. "And if people see you play, we'll get more joiners than the debate team."

"Next time for sure."

Mandi taps the board with her pen. *Rap-rap-rap.* Pause. *Rap-rap-rap.* "Christopher, would you please excuse us? Oscar and I have something to discuss."

Chess boy skitters away, but a boy wearing a physics club T-shirt steps in the space he left behind. Mandi gives him a look and he's gone, too.

"We have to take action," she says.

"I can't talk," I tell her. "There's an emergency." Chess boy ate up at least four of my precious minutes to find the girl.

"Of course there's an emergency. Our beautiful town has been defaced."

I give her what she wants so she'll let me go. "It's shocking. Horrible. Beyond belief."

"I saved the top spot on the petition for you." Mandi shoves the clipboard at me. When I don't take it fast enough, she wraps my fingers around the pen. The only time she touches me is when she wants me to do something.

Mandi asked me out two years ago. "We're the smartest kids in class," she said. "We should date. Not that I'm bragging—one should never brag about one's own accomplishments."

"Why not?" I said. Having a perfect girlfriend was just another layer for the disguise.

So I take her to dances, and we sit together in study hall. Sometimes we go out for ice cream. She likes to have her own fro-yo sundae. No sharing. We get along fine.

She's intense, even with her brain soaked in Messages. Usually it's entertaining, but today she's in my way.

"Here." I give the signed petition back and step to the left. I have to find her.

Mandi matches my step, so we're still facing each other. "Take the board and get it signed. I have plenty."

"Then can I go?"

She nods. "Fifty signatures by lunch. Um, I mean, please try. Always ask for favors nicely." Mandi looks frustrated with herself. It must be hard having both the Messages and her bossy self inside one brain. "But I really need fifty."

I put her out of her misery. "I promise."

People are moving faster now. Almost time to be where you're supposed to go. We all know the great are never late.

Mandi slips into the stream without saying good-bye.

"Oscar! Do you want to be my lab partner today?" It's the girl who sits in front of me in chemistry. Her curly brown ponytail looks highly flammable. Sometimes I wonder what would happen if I tilted my burner toward her. . . .

"If you think you can keep up." I give her a small wink to feed the persona. "No, seriously, it would be my honor."

She blushes as if I just suggested making out under the lab table. "Okay, um, well, see you there!"

Before another worshipper can approach, I see skateboarding girl at the end of the hall. Black T-shirt and tangled hair, in the middle of smooth-headed clones wearing pastel. Beautiful and dangerous.

I push through the crowd.

"Oscar! I'm having an SAT review party Saturday—"

"Can't." I push past.

Black T-shirt, straight ahead but moving fast. I up my pace.

Some interchangeable girl steps in front of me. "Is that a petition? May I sign it?"

I toss it to the beggar. "Keep it and get fifty more."

I almost lose her. For a second, it's only pastel and blank faces, but then she turns a corner and I catch a glimpse. A black cloud in a blue sky.

"Oscar, heads up!" Some idiot tosses me a baseball, like I'm his hallway shortstop. I bat it aside.

I've almost caught up. Now I totally ignore the kids talking, begging, kissing my butt. Rude is okay right now. My disguise doesn't matter.

Talking to *her* matters.

Finally I get close. When she sees me, a slow smile stretches her mouth open. "Good morning, Picasso."

"Don't call me that. Don't even think it." I step so close, her nose almost touches my chin. My lips buzz with possibility.

Her smile fades and she tilts up her face. For a crazy second I think we'll kiss, but then she takes a step back. "Scared I'll tell?"

"We'd both be screwed." The kids around us slow and stare.

I glance at my watch. "The great are never late." The classic makes them nod and get moving again, away from hearing something that could get me in trouble.

"I have geology." She tries to step back again, but the hall is too full and she stumbles.

I grab her before she can fall. I don't let go. "I know it's in your head. You think you have to tell. It's like an itch, right?"

"Nobody knows what's in my head." Her eyes are wet. "Nobody's invited."

"Invite me." I don't mean it to sound cheesy, but it does.

"Spare me." When she pulls her arm away, I don't stop her. "That line can't even work on the baby dolls here."

"You're not like them. That's a good thing." I'm late. Worried.

But she still tempts me.

She laughs. "Unlike you. It's like you were made to match them."

"Matching is boring." I find my eyes on her lips again. No. Focus. Those lips could tell the truth. Get me in trouble.

I look at the lockers over her head. Cold. Metal. Like my brain should be right now. "You shouldn't tell."

"You shouldn't have stolen the paint." She arches an eyebrow.

"Don't act like it's all my fault. You practically dared me."

"I told you to give it back. But you had to pretend you were a big bad boy." A grin transforms her mouth to new lusciousness—then it's gone. "Maybe you should be punished."

How can I stop her? I close my eyes for a second. The Message is there, waiting. Then I see the loophole. "You don't have to tell today."

"Why not?"

"Because girls like you don't rat. You're better than that." I don't know if I'm right. But I hope I am. I want her to be that girl.

She gives a tiny shrug, bounces a little on her toes, and wraps her arms around herself. "You might be a little bit right."

"Just wait until we can talk more. Please." If I can get some time, I can make my own Message, something that will make sure she'll keep my secret. Something that will keep her interesting, too. Until I can get her out of here, far away from anyone she can tell my secret to.

"Are you going to charm me like all the other acolytes?" she asks.

"Nice SAT word." My cute-boy smile hits my face. A reflex. "Just come to the model homes on Sunday. I'll be working in the Roxbury from ten until four. We'll talk."

"Fine. Okay." She shakes her head like she's disagreeing with herself. "If it's not raining or anything."

14

The bell rings. We're both late. I walk one way. She goes the other. At least I know why I'm hurrying. She has no idea.

Two days of holding my breath. I wish it were sooner. But I need somewhere safe to talk to her, a place where nobody who matters will see us.

I'll have to risk it. I'll have to hope she's rebel enough—or that some part of her wants to pick me instead of the words in her head.

The smart thing would be to run away.

But I've got promises to keep here. And I've always beat the Messages before.

But will she?

chapter 3

CANDOR IS MY dad's dream come true. He bought a chunk of Florida swamp, far away from highways and cities. Planned a town with big houses on tiny lots. It would be old fashioned, a place where you left the door unlocked and knew all your neighbors. Potlucks and lemonade stands galore.

For years, my mother said he was crazy. Nobody would buy. We'd go broke. But after Winston's funeral, she lost all her fight. Dad broke ground and we left Chicago.

Now it costs a million dollars to live here. There's a two-year waiting list just to buy one of those tiny lots. It takes another year to get a house built—if you're lucky.

Mom's gone now, but everyone else wants to live here.

On Sundays, I work in the model homes, handing out brochures. Smile bright. Casually mention the Ivy League recruiters that show up every fall.

I don't mind helping. Potential clients are always walking through the door. There's no way I can mine from the kids born here: there's no room for bad in their brains. It was never even invented for them.

You never see a tantrum here. Not unless the kid's new.

Without new families, my business would dry up. Rich parents drag in a pissed-off kid with fancy electronics hanging from his designer jeans pockets. I make nice. See if he's got access to his own funds—or if Mommy and Daddy have it locked up.

If the kid can offer something interesting, it helps their odds. I like gadgets. Goodies. Girls with a major hotness quotient. My clients also have to be old enough to survive on their own. Once they're gone there's no phoning home for help.

Today won't be about finding new clients, though. I'll be waiting for skateboarding girl to show up. I burnt her a special CD with my own Messages—ones to keep *me* safe.

I just have to find a way to get her to listen.

I did some research after our beloved town founder went to bed in his monogrammed linen pajamas. Nia Silva, 17, from Boston. She hates school and loves running away. Her last time, she vanished for a week and came home with habits and a nasty disease. That's when her parents got the lucky call: they were off the waiting list. In two days they had bought their four-bedroom Victorian on Magnolia Court.

Now that I know about her, I'm in control again.

But first I have my chores, like every Candor kid.

"Be sure not to burn the rye." Dad pulls the business section out of the Sunday paper, all the way from Chicago. It's been seven years since we left the city but he still likes to keep up.

"I thought I'd make waffles instead." It's my Sunday fantasy: brunch. With cinnamon rolls and crispy bacon that leaves shiny strips of grease on the plates. There would be eggs, too, cooked in lots of butter.

"Very funny." He slurps up a mouthful of coffee.

I'm never late. The Messages make sure of that. But today I want to be early to work. I don't want to miss her.

I jam the bread in the toaster. Two pieces for him, two pieces for me. Nothing more is allowed. Nothing more, Dad would say, is needed.

Dad brags that his son cooks and does the laundry and vacuums twice a week. People don't need cleaning ladies in Candor—they have their kids.

It happens fast. One day kids are blasting their music, ignoring their parents, smoking or drinking or doing whatever they're not supposed to.

And then, they're dusting. Cooking dinner. Making their beds every morning. As long as it doesn't interfere with homework.

I've watched 1,381 families move in. Thousands of kids, all changing to fit the same ideal.

But it's not just the kids. Candor fixes everything.

Do you smoke? We'll fix it. Got marital problems? Prepare for bliss. Undermotivated? Overeating? Can't get it up? It will all go away in just a few weeks.

Everyone is saturated with Messages from the day they move in. Speakers are installed in bushes downtown, at the parks, in the stores—not just school. And then parents play special custom "boosters" at home. Even send them off in care packages to their darlings at college. Candor kids only go to certain colleges, with certain accommodations: special dorms and classes. Music and speakers everywhere they go. Anything is possible with enough money.

You can't hear the Messages—or at least, you don't realize you're listening. They're subliminal. That means your subconscious hears them. And it obeys.

I hear all the same Messages. But I know how to make new ones. I make my own playlists with jazz music—Coltrane, Bird—and hidden commands. I play them when I'm sleeping:

Remember the Messages.

Control the Messages; don't let them control you.

Think independently.

It helps. My brain tells me what I'm supposed to do, but I can fight it, usually. I pick my battles, conserve my energy.

"What do you know about this graffiti?"

Dad's voice is even. His eyes are steady on me. I have to be careful. What I'm supposed to do pulses in my brain. *Tell, tell, tell.*

"I heard it was orange." I think about nothing. Empty brain. Empty eyes. Keep them on him. Not staring. Just unknowing.

Unafraid.

"Speaking of orange, how about some juice?" Dad asks.

Turning away is a relief, even though I feel him watching and thinking. I've developed a sense for it.

I get out two glasses and a bottle of orange juice. The fridge is hidden behind cherry cabinet panels. Before the models were built, people toured our house. Everything is top-of-the-line.

"Careful," he warns. "Just six ounces."

After you lose ninety-three pounds, you watch what you eat. And if you're Campbell Banks, you watch what everyone else eats, too. This town runs on dry toast and egg whites. And they like it.

He's making me nervous, quizzing and watching. But it's good news. It means she didn't talk. I'm safe, if I can keep him in the dark. I'm good at that.

"Better hurry. Models open in ten minutes." Dad's eyes slide to my empty chair. A command I obey.

Two bites and my toast is gone. I gulp down my juice. It's not enough. Not even close.

"Reverend Able says some boys from Okeechobee must have left the graffiti," he says.

I blink once. Twice. "Why would anyone want to do that? Our community should stay beautiful." That's another phrase I've been noticing a lot since that night, lapping at the edge of my thoughts.

"Not everyone gets the message." Dad snaps off a tiny piece of toast.

Message. Every time he says it, I get nervous. I look into my empty glass before he can notice. "I hope you find out soon," I say.

The Messages rush in right away. *Never lie to your parents. Always be truthful.* But those are old ones, and it's not hard to push them back.

Dad stands up. He rinses the rye seeds off his plate and opens the dishwasher. "Keep your ears open."

"I hear everything," I say. He likes to think I'm his little spy.

The scary part is over. My stomach rumbles. I reach for the juice and hope he won't notice.

"No more today." Dad picks up a pencil from the pad by the phone. Then he marks the juice line on the bottle. There's a stack of lines above it.

It's nothing new, but today it makes me angry just when I should keep my mouth shut. "I'm still thirsty."

"You got enough." He taps the side of the bottle. "One serving. Have some water."

"Yes, sir." Everything is just-enough in our house. He weighs the meat before I cook it. Our beds have one blanket and one pillow.

Luxury is for other people. Weak people who pay Dad money for it.

He points at the door with the eraser end of the pencil. "You'll be late."

The great are never late. The Message washes across my mind and my fear rides on top of them. I let it push my feet out the door.

chapter 4

I GET TO the Roxbury two minutes late. Put my key in the door. Then I look at my watch and wait.

Every day I test myself a different way. I know what I'm supposed to do. It's fed to my brain 24/7. But I resist. I have to make sure I can do it. I have to know, for when it really matters.

Three minutes late. Four.

The Message pounds in my head: *The great are never late. The great are never late.* It's a tough one to fight: It plays every day. Everywhere. One of Dad's classics.

"You don't own me," I mutter. I do what I want.

Sweat rolls off my nose and drops on the toe of my fresh-shined dress shoes. My teeth are clenched. I force my jaw to relax and look at my watch again. There. Five minutes late. That's enough.

Before I go in, I look down the street. Is she coming? But I don't see her. No *ca-chunk, ca-chunk* skateboard sound, either.

"Relax," I tell myself. Nobody breaks a date with Oscar Banks.

I go inside and check the fridge. Sometimes there's oatmeal cookie dough to bake. It makes the house smell good and it's a lot tastier than rye toast. But not today. Just miniature bottles of spring water with the Candor seal stamped on the caps.

I crack one open and sit on the edge of the bench in the break-fast nook. My legs won't stop bouncing, twitching. I hate this girl for making me wait.

My mother made the cushions and curtains for the first model homes. This one had red cushions and gold curtains. But when she was gone, those vanished overnight, too. Now the cushion has little palm trees and monkeys on it. Just like the curtains and the pillow shams in the master bedroom. Very tropical.

But if you look outside, you'd never know it was Florida. Palm trees are outlawed in Candor, unless they grow in a nature preserve. Instead there are oaks and pines. Makes everyone feel at home, Dad says. It's like we could be anywhere.

Instead of the middle of nowhere.

Candor boasts six stunning model homes, with designer up-grades and don't-miss landscaping. That's what the brochure says. The Roxbury is my favorite. It features double porches, granite coun-tertops, and a potting shed out back. The old people go crazy for the potting shed.

I like it, too. The door has a lock on the inside. There are shades that blot out light at night. And it's got an electric outlet for my laptop.

I meet with all my clients there.

My father has no idea that he built me an office right in the backyard of his best-selling model. He thinks he controls me. But I know all the loopholes. I even invented some of them.

The front door opens and the alarm system softly *beep-beep-beeps*. I jump up, then sit down so fast the bench hurts me.

Let her come to me. I need to keep control, own the situation.

A tall fat kid with a stained T-shirt walks in. He takes a long slurp from the jumbo soda cup in his meaty hand.

"I can't believe the soda machines only have juice. Since when is apple juice supposed to taste like Coke?" he asks.

Sherman. My only client, for now. Needy. Nervous. Rich. He's the last thing I need to deal with right now.

"Did I say you could come here?" I ask.

Always be courteous. The Message pokes at me. I run my fingers over my head and grip my hair, as if I can pull the Message out through my scalp. If only it were that easy.

"Persistence pays off," Sherman says.

That's a Message. Something I shouldn't be hearing him say, unless he's trying to be ironic. Which I don't think he's capable of.

"Are you listening to the stuff I gave you?" My booster music should be keeping him strong, but if he's spouting Messages, it's not working. He'll be a goner in a few days.

"Of course I am. I'm good at following directions. But the saxophone music sucks." He opens the fridge and looks inside.

I wonder if I should push his exit date up, but my driver's hard to reach. And he doesn't take kindly to change.

But I can't worry about Sherman, not right now. I have to be ready for Nia, which means ditching him.

"Get out," I tell Sherman. "I'm working."

"I gave you all my money. You work for *me*." He plants his butt on the counter. Sweaty Sherman pudge pressing against Dad's favorite Brazilian granite. It would be kind of funny if I didn't want to kill him.

Beep-beep-beep. Someone else is here. Not her, please. Not until I've de-Shermaned the place.

A kid in denim overalls streaks past me, headed straight for the bathroom. Not good. Kids always like to throw things in the toilets.

"Don't talk to anyone. Don't touch anything." I give him a

I'm-not-kidding look before I walk to the front hallway.

There's a family in the dining room, touching all the china place settings on the table: tired Mommy, flush-faced Daddy, and three short sticky kids, not counting the escapee in the powder room. I look for labels on the brats' overalls. Nothing. They're from Wal-Mart, maybe, or some other affordable, durable brand.

"You must be lost," I say. "Public restrooms are in the Brighton."

The daddy wanders past me into the kitchen. Sherman territory. I follow.

"Welcome to Candor!" Sherman gives him a cheery wave. "Have you met Oscar? He's a genius. An evil genius." He lets out a high-pitched giggle.

I was worried about his chattiness when I approached him and offered to save him. But I'd seen his bank balance—all the buyers have to give that information to my father, including their kids' accounts—and I knew he could be worth my time.

I quoted him the total amount in his account. He didn't even blink. Things were slow and the kid was throwing major bucks at me. Why not?

Now I know why not.

"Who's Oscar?" the man asks.

"Nobody." I hand him a price sheet. "I'm guessing you can't afford this place."

He looks at the sheet. His eyebrows jerk up and down. "Lorna. Where's Ella?" he barks.

Mommy shrugs. She's kid-free. What does she care?

I hear a toilet flush. "Sounds like a priceless figurine going down the potty," I say. "You break it, you buy it."

"Kids! Don't touch anything!" Daddy runs off.

Mommy sighs. "What pretty music."

Pretty like a Venus flytrap. The subliminal messages play at a frequency so low that you can't hear them, but part of your brain does. Stay at the Roxbury long enough and you'll be convinced that the houses are worth every penny.

Sherman pipes up again. "If you're smart, you'll plug your ears." He jams his fingers in his ears and crosses his eyes.

I walk over to him and stand so the woman can't see what I'm doing. Then I pinch his knee, right above the kneecap. "Shut up or leave," I whisper.

When I turn around, the woman's stuffing brochures in her purse.

"We don't supply arts-and-crafts paper for the kids." I hold out my hand. She gives me a dirty look and hands back half.

"Let's go, kids," she shouts. "We're not wanted here."

"Took you a long time to figure that out." I give her my sweetest smile.

And they go.

I turn to Sherman. "What's wrong with you? Do you remember what I said?"

He rolls his eyes. "No talking about secret stuff. Listen to the music you gave me. Never talk to you in front of witnesses."

"Don't even make eye contact. Didn't I say that?" My voice is loud, but it doesn't matter. There's nobody to hear except Sherman.

"But I have questions. And I'm bored." He swings his legs and his heels bounce off the cherry cabinets.

"Stop. Scuffs." I grab a paper towel and rub at the white marks his sneakers left behind.

"For someone who's fighting the system, you sure care a lot about this place."

I feel a surge of irritation. I can't wait for this kid to be gone from this house. And my town. "My dad needs to think I'm perfect."

And the Messages have a few things to say about keeping houses clean and not destroying property. But I don't admit I'm listening to those.

"So what should I pack?" he asks. "What will I need?"

Things I don't usually discuss too far ahead. I tell them the night before. But I'd do almost anything to get rid of him.

"If I answer your questions, will you leave?" I ask.

He shrugs. "Maybe."

I stare until he lets out a gusty sigh. "Fine. Definitely," he says.

"Pack light," I tell him. "It's a long walk through the woods to the edge of town. You only need a change of clothes and your iPod. Make sure it's loaded with the music I gave you."

I give my clients Messages to listen to when they leave. I have to. Once you start listening to the Messages, you can never stop. Not when you go to college, or on a business trip, or even an overnight to visit Grandma Bee in Sarasota.

Dad didn't just build the first brainwashing community—he invented a new kind of addiction: aural addiction, he calls it. Everybody in Candor is hooked on the Messages, including the parents who paid big money to be here. Nobody leaves town without headphones and their special music.

Without them, the withdrawal will kill you.

"Who's meeting me?" Sherman asks.

"A white truck will pull up. You'll get in."

My driver, Frank, runs a critter-trapping service. Dad's people call him all the time about gators, water moccasins, anything that scares our hardy citizens. I like to think he removes all kinds of pests from town.

apter 5

ND HER the next day at lunch. She's sitting alone at Founder's
, across from the school. It's not hard to spot her. Black jeans,
k tank top. Probably not even her panties are pastel.

I wave, but she doesn't see me. She's staring at the notebook in
lap, like every other kid at the park. Has she changed since we
ed?

Founder's Park is like the library, only with ants and ninety-degree
at. It's where all the super-duper-achievers come at lunch. They
ew carrot sticks and memorize theorems at the same time.

They all sit alone. The broad triangle of grass is dotted with
em, surrounded with piles of books and binders and highlighters.
he ones who didn't score a shady spot wear hats with big brims.
ways protect yourself from the sun.

Nobody stops me as I walk by. Sure, a few look up and give me
wave like we're best friends. But that's easy to deal with. I smile.
Vave back. Give them a thumbs-up.

I should come here more often. It's the only public place I get
eft alone.

More nods. More waves. I smile and keep moving toward my
arget.

My clients sit in the back with the cages. It's not luxury, but
Frank is rock-solid reliable. He'd never turn me in. I pay 50 percent
more than Dad. In cash.

"Where will the truck take me?"

"The truck takes you far, far away from me. So we like the truck,"
I tell him. "We like it a lot."

His cheeks tremble. "Why are you so mean to me? I see you at
school. You're all smiling and talking to other people."

"I'm—not." But he's right. I *am* mean to him. And I'm fake with
everyone else. For a minute, I feel bad for him. Poor slob. He doesn't
deserve being here. All he did was be his nasty, farting, burping self—
someone his sleek parents couldn't live with.

But then he opens his mouth and talks again. "The customer is
always right. You should be nice. You should be kissing my butt."

Sherman makes it impossible to be nice. "You're *my* customer?"
I snarl it. Step close. "You think I owe *you*?"

He crosses his arms and leans back. "Don't be mad."

The Messages fill my brain, like boulders sliding down a chute.
Never threaten someone's safety. Respectful space in every place. I feel
my fists relaxing. I draw in a deep breath.

The door beeps again.

"Get out." I point at the back door. "I answered all your questions."

He wipes the back of his hand over his eyes. Sniffles. I rush to
the front hall.

A bald man wearing a golf visor is standing with his hands on his
hips, staring up at the thousand-dollar light in the entryway.

"My kid's shrink said we should come here," he says.

Which makes him what Dad calls a *qualified* candidate. Candor's big secret is marketed quietly: discreet chatter at rich people's

cocktail parties, referrals from happy customers. And suggestions from well-paid psychiatrists.

If his financials check out, Dad will tell him what he'd really be buying.

"How much?" the man asks.

I hand him the price sheet from the dining room table. "Starting at one-point-two. Before upgrades."

"Not bad," he says. Like he's debating whether to supersize his lunch.

I slide open a drawer in the table and pull out one of the DVDs. "Watch this. You'll learn all about the benefits that Candor has to offer."

I used to feel bad, helping to sell the houses. But I was stuck. I knew Dad was using the Messages to make me work there, so I smiled and handed out floor plans. Told everyone how great the schools are.

I'd look at kids walking in. Poor suckers, I'd think. You have no idea what's about to hit you.

House sales started breaking records. The waiting list grew: six months. A year. Two years. Every house sold for more money. Nobody leaves here, so the only option is to buy from my dad. I realized I couldn't stop what was happening. All I could do was protect myself. Maybe help a few others. That was all.

"Thanks for your help, son." The man shakes my hand. His grip is firm.

Now comes the part where I show him the house. Point out the vaulted ceilings and voice-activated bedroom lights. But then I hear something through the open front door.

Ca-chunk, ca-chunk, ca-chunk.

"Be sure to check out the home theater." I point upstairs.

His eyebrows twitch up and down. Rich
blowoff. "Granite come standard?" he asks.

"It's all on the price sheet." Dad would b

The sound stops. And now I hear somet
voice. Two voices. Sherman is talking to her
happening.

Baldy is saying something about financing
cies. Why am I being nice to him? He's not im

Always be courteous. The Message is far
brain has been bathing in it for a long time. Th
it owns me.

No, I tell it. *My brain is mine.*

"We're closed." I point at the door.

Baldy just stares.

"Fire drill. State law. Sorry." I force my feet
to push him out, even if my body fights me.

But he goes. I slam the door shut and run bac
It's empty.

Sherman is gone. But so is whoever he was tall

Then I hear it again. The sound of a skatebo
front and onto the sidewalk. The sound is quieter . .

And then she's gone.

It's good I missed her yesterday. I was desperate. Stupid. But I'm prepared now.

Dad taught me that good salespeople customize their message. I plan on listening to his advice.

I reach in my backpack and turn my player on. Music filters through the canvas. I thumb the volume lower. It'll be easier if she doesn't notice it. This music is only for her subconscious—and my safety.

The only way to protect myself is to tell her the truth. Then she won't turn down my special music—she'll beg for it. I'll make sure she never tells about the graffiti. Maybe even get her to pay for the privilege before I give her a nudge out of town.

She'll be like any other client.

Everyone reacts differently when I tell them. Some kids don't believe me, not right away. Others—the ones that I caught too late—just don't care. Then there are the believers. They tend to freak out. Let's call the *New York Times*, they say. Or, they tell me they have an uncle/sister/old teacher back home who will help. Usually there's talk of yelling at Mommy and Daddy.

When I tell the potentials, the believers are the dangerous ones. If they squeal, my father would find out someone's been spreading the news. One phone call from a reporter or a relative or the believer's mommy would expose everything I've been hiding. Dad might pay off a reporter, but he'd still find the source: me.

Then he'd know the truth: I'm not his dream son. I'm the opposite. He'd send me to the Listening Room. That'd fix me, for good.

I've survived too long. I won't let some random kid mess it up for me.

So I always bring my insurance. Maybe it sounds like elevator music, but it's got special Messages, too. Instructions that stop people from telling. Instructions that keep them calm.

I threw in a little something about graffiti and secrets, too. Just for her.

"I hope you're not studying." I sit down without being asked and nudge the backpack close to her.

She looks up for a second. "You again. Go away."

"You wanted to talk to me yesterday."

She shrugs. "I was weak."

"Why'd you leave without talking to me?"

"Something more interesting came up." A smile flickers over her face. She licks her lips. A revolting picture involving Sherman's blubber and her tongue pops into my head.

"Did Sherman tell you to leave?"

"Sherman. Is that his name? It fits." Another flick of her tongue. My cheeks feel hot.

"Don't bother with Sherman. He's nobody."

"You and me—we're not buddies now," she says.

"I wasn't—I'm not—" But part of me wants something besides fixing things. She's interesting. Someone real.

"You're just the jerk who stole my paint," she says.

"You mean the paint *you* stole?"

She rolls her head around her shoulders, like she's loosening up for a fight. "It was mine when you took it, and you wasted it. Now you're stalking me."

"I don't stalk." People come to me.

"I haven't decided when I'll tell," she says.

"How about never?" Is the music in my backpack loud enough? I need her to listen to it as long as possible and then I need her to take my CDs.

"You can go now. In fact, you'd better. What if blondie finds you?"

"You mean Mandi?" So she's been doing some research, too. "I don't care if she sees me."

Nia makes a shooing motion. But me and my backpack are staying. I point at the notebook in her lap. It's so big it covers both her knees. There aren't any lines on the paper. "What's that for?"

She snorts. "*Please* tell me you've seen a sketch pad before."

I feel stupid. Why? Why do I care what she thinks? She's the one who should worry about what I think. I'm her ticket out of town.

"There aren't many sketch pads around here," I say.

Dad's hated art since Mom left. Art is a waste of time, he says. And he makes sure that's what everyone else thinks, too. But I try not to. I remember how beautiful Mom's pottery was.

"Another thing to hate about this place." Nia balls up both fists and rubs them into her eyes. "There's not one lousy art class."

The morning after Mom left, Dad gathered up all her pots and plates and the little zoo of animals she had made for my fifth birthday. Took them outside. And chucked them at the fence, one by one. Mom leaving must have hurt more than ignoring the Messages that he should have heard, telling him to stop.

I didn't stop him. I was angry, too. This was what she deserved, I thought. She'd come back and see how much she hurt us.

But she didn't come back.

When he was done, he made me clean up. I saved a piece, yellow with brown spots. I think it was part of a giraffe. I put it in my desk drawer. Sometimes the sharp edges scrape me when I reach for a pencil or my calculator.

They remind me not to trust anyone. It's like Dad says. Everyone leaves.

So I might as well profit from it.

I launch the usual speech. "I have a proposal," I say. "Well—you know. Not that kind of proposal. Not going to Vegas or anything. A deal. I want to make a deal with you."

It's coming out all wrong. How does she do that? How does she make my mouth open and let out words that don't make sense? I've given this speech a million times. That's not how it's supposed to start.

But she doesn't seem to hear me. She's running one finger over her sketch pad. The other hand reaches up to tuck a stray hair behind her ear. She glances up at me. Looks back at the pad.

"To start, I have to tell you something shocking," I say. Good. Back on track.

"Shh." She circles a pencil over the pad. But it doesn't touch the paper. Just circles. Floats down, almost touches. Flies up. Circles again. It looks like a bird that doesn't know how to stop flying.

"You might not believe me at first. But I promise it's true."

More pencil circling. More ignoring me.

I check my watch. Just twelve minutes before the bell. Sixteen minutes before physics. "Listen to me," I tell her.

"Dammit!" Now she balls her hand into a fist and slams it on the pad. "I'm trying to concentrate."

I bet it wasn't always this hard for her. "You're forgetting how to do it, aren't you?" I ask.

"I'm just having a hard time getting started. It happens."

Sure. It wouldn't be those Messages that are seeping in, telling her there are more important things to be doing. "It happens to all the arty kids who move to Candor," I tell her. "Eventually they give up."

Her eyes dart to meet mine then go back to her empty pad. "That doesn't really happen, does it?"

"It's true. In a week, you won't even care about drawing or painting. Unless . . ."

"Stop. Just stop talking." Now her voice is loud and certain again. She jabs her pencil toward me. "And don't move."

"But I can help you." I have to.

"Shut up. Sit still. Or go." She jerks her head back toward the school.

The breeze shifts. Her hair blows around her face. I smell something sweet. Lilacs. They used to grow outside our kitchen door in Chicago. But it's too hot for them here. I breathe in deep.

"You get three minutes," I tell her. "Then I talk, and you listen."

"I've got it now," she mutters. Her hand swoops over her sketch pad. It's not a lost bird anymore. Now it's graceful. Certain. The pencil leaves dark arcs and lines behind. They don't look like anything yet. But I can tell she has a plan.

She looks up at me. Squints.

"Like what you see?" I wiggle my eyebrows.

"Silence." But a corner of her mouth twitches up just for a second. Then she's back to drawing.

Not many people order me around. There's my dad—and I guess my teachers, if you count assignments as orders. But the kids at school respect me. Vote for me when I run for elections. Sometimes even when I don't. Last year I won Class President on a write-in.

The church bell bongs noon. Just seven minutes until the bell. I have to tell her. The music I'm playing now won't be enough—she needs lots more.

"It's my turn," I tell her.

"One more minute. Don't talk." She picks her pencil off the paper and moves it toward my face. I watch it come closer until I'm cross-eyed.

Then she touches the eraser to the bottom of my lip. Drags it slowly around the edge of my mouth. It feels gritty, but soft. Gentle.

"There," she whispers. "Now I've got the shape."

She pulls it away fast and starts drawing again. My lips tingle. I want her to do it again.

No. She's running the show. That has to stop.

"My turn." I slap my hand over the drawing.

She looks up. "There are better places to put that hand."

I let myself imagine. One lucky hand, set loose. No boundaries. I shiver. "Where do you want me to start?" I say.

A Candor girl would spew a few Messages at me if I tried that. Probably walk away as fast as she could, once she was done reminding me how good she was. But Nia just pokes my hand off the paper with her pencil eraser and goes back to drawing.

Then I remember: I have to make this fast and convincing. So I start at the end of my usual speech. "They're brainwashing you," I say. "Soon there won't be anything special left."

She snorts and glances up. "And here I thought you were all robots. Robots can do all kinds of interesting things, you know."

"It's not a joke. People are perfect here because of the Messages."

"You have points on the tips of your ears." She tilts her head and stares at me. "Like a big, tall elf."

"You have to listen to me." I hear my voice getting loud, like it's some other guy talking. Some guy who can't control himself. "Or you won't be drawing anymore. You'll be just like them."

"Now that's scary." But she's still smiling as she sketches.

The bell rings. Four minutes. I feel the urge to hurry. "You don't have long," I tell her. "Usually it only takes a week, maybe two. Unless you let me help you."

"The great are never late! We must go inside quickly!" A familiar voice. Familiar spotless white sneakers. Socks with white lace around the ankles. I look up. Yes. It's Mandi.

"Oscar?" She looks at Nia, then back at me. "You never come to Founder's Park."

Mandi is a Founder's Park regular, especially when there's a test coming up. And there's almost always a test coming up.

"It was a nice day out," I lie. It's hot, like always. I feel the sweat running down my back, but I feel like I owe her a lie.

Nia shades her eyes and looks up. "Are you his nanny?"

It doesn't dent Mandi's smile. "You must be new here. I'm Mandi Able. President of the Welcome Club. Did you like your basket?"

"I hate bananas. They're so yellow and cheerful." Nia leans back on her hands, like she's settling in. Not like she's got a class in two minutes.

"Well, but there was a lot more than . . . fruit. . . ." Mandi bites her lip and looks at the school.

"Maybe you'd better get to class, Mandi." Nia gives me a wink. As if I'm going to stay sitting here with her, which I won't. I can't. People would see. And I never, ever, blow my cover.

I stand up.

Mandi holds her hand out to me. "Come on, honey. We have to hurry."

Honey. She hardly ever calls me that. It's sentimental and Mandi's too busy for that. Why did she have to pull it out today? I feel like a kindergartner whose mother just showed up at the playground with spare underpants.

I don't take her hand. I reach in my backpack and turn off the music. Then I feel the CDs. I can't go without giving them to Nia.

"Take these." I drop them by her feet. She meets my eyes. For a second, it feels like we're alone again.

"A present? For *me*?" Nia bats her eyes at Mandi. "How sweet. Sweet like honey."

Mandi balls her fists up, just for a second. When they relax, her back gets even straighter.

Before Mandi moved here, she was the queen of the teen beauty pageant circuit. She wasn't just pretty, she was . . . determined. She'd do anything, say anything, to win. None of the adults knew how bad it was until something went wrong. Miss Hidalgo County killed herself and left a note blaming Mandi. It's embarrassing for a preacher's daughter to tease a kid to death. Her parents decided she needed a change of attitude.

And now she's just the queen nerd. She's forgotten how to be mean, at least most of the time.

Mandi folds her arms. "Oscar didn't mention he was working on a class project with you, either."

"He isn't." Nia slaps her notebook shut and stands up.

It looks like Mandi wants to say something, but it's stuck inside her mouth. So she just flicks her bangs back and looks at me. "Ready to go?"

They're both staring at me. I lean down, slowly, to pick up my backpack. The CDs are on the grass.

I hold them out, breaking my own rule. Never talk to a client about business in public. And definitely not in front of a witness. Especially a curious, slightly unstable one.

"Promise me you'll listen," I say.

Because I need to protect her.

Because some of my Messages will make sure she stays this interesting.

Nia takes them.

"See you later, *honey.*" Nia gives me a fake smile, almost as bright as Mandi's. "Thanks for the gifties."

She takes off, fast, almost jogging. Not headed for school.

"You're going the wrong way," Mandi shouts.

Nia flips us the bird and keeps on going.

"I guess she already knew that," I say.

The second bell rings. We are officially late.

"We're late," she whispers. "We're in trouble."

"I'm sorry. I'll tell Ms. Russo it was my fault." I start toward school.

But she grabs my elbow to stop me. "This is the part where you say nice things to make me feel better."

I'm not the best boyfriend, seeing as how Mandi bores me to death. But she's been useful. I owe her something, I think. "It was nothing," I say. "We were just talking. The CDs are a thing for my psych class. It's not like she's pretty. Or smart, like you."

She gives me a funny look. "I mean about getting detention."

"Oh. Right." So I spend the rest of the walk to class telling her how great detention is. It's like study hall. It doesn't go on your permanent record. And it's really, really quiet so you can concentrate on flash cards and writing brilliant admissions essays.

Not that I would know. I've never been there, either.

I only look over my shoulder once, maybe twice. Wondering where Nia went.

Wishing I'd had the guts to go with her.

Wishing I'd been invited.

chapter 6

I CAN'T STOP thinking about Nia. Her hand swooping, drawing. The lilac smell of her hair. How she walked away from school without even looking back.

It's like she's become a Message, stuck in my brain. I hate it. But I want it. Just by existing, she's controlling me.

This has to be fixed.

After dinner, I give Dad the usual lie. "I'm going to the library."

"Be home by ten," he says.

It's that easy to sneak out. Sometimes being brainwashed is useful. Dad is sure that I would never lie to him or do anything naughty.

When I get to the Roxbury, I go in through the backyard. There are still lights on in the house: kitchen, dining nook, and one of the bedrooms upstairs. Nobody's inside. Dad just likes to make it look that way. The lights are programmed to change every two hours.

But the shed is dark. I guess nobody in Dad's fantasy world gardens in the dark.

The key is under the ladybug doormat, like always. I only use one electric lantern, and I keep the blinds shut. From the outside you can't tell someone is here.

The shed feels like a real place, where somebody actually gardens and arranges flowers and hangs them to dry from the rafters.

It's bigger than anything called a shed deserves to be. There's room for a tall wood table in the middle, twice the length of our dining room table. There are two sinks: one for mixing fertilizer, or washing your shovels, or whatever gardeners do. The other is supposed to be for arranging flowers. There are pots and a pair of scissors sitting by that one and some fake half-arranged flowers. I keep two sets of earphones in that vase, beneath the wire stems.

Below the counters are bins and buckets of all sizes and colors. Handy for hiding things, like my portable DVD player.

Tonight I pull out a metal bin. The recorder is inside. My thumb rests easily on the button. I know exactly what I'm going to tell myself to do.

Why waste time? I press the button down, but my lips are glued shut. They won't let the words through.

Nia Silva is boring. Ignore her. Six short words. Smart ones.

I've made plenty of Messages for myself. Why does this one have to be so hard?

My first was about Winston. *Winston was your big brother.* I knew Dad wanted me to forget. But I wouldn't let him do that to me—or Winston. I still listen to that Message sometimes. Just to be sure.

I try again. "Nia is—" But that's all I can get out.

Maybe I need something to make me less jittery. I walk to the back wall and tug on a seam in the glossy white paneling.

The panel swings open to reveal my stash. Devil Dogs and Pop-Tarts, stored in plastic containers so the ants can't get them. Gum—strictly forbidden in Candor. There's a pile of tasty movies and magazines, and some video games with buxom chicks. Then I run my finger over the bottle collection. Pick my favorite and uncap. Pour liberally.

"Cheers." I tip my cup to the hardworking ladies in my magazine collection and take a seat. There are two Adirondack chairs tucked in a corner by the door. Like gardening is so exhausting, there's no way you could make it back to the house. There's a pair of orange rubber shoes sitting at the base of one of the chairs. It feels like they belong to someone.

I take a gulp. Hit the button.

"Nia Silva is . . ."

Boring? The opposite. I wonder what would happen if she were here, sitting in the chair next to me. No, in my chair. Ready and willing. Straddling me. Leaning close. Flowery silky hair touching my face . . .

The memory of my father's warning cracks the fantasy open like a hammer on an egg.

Everyone leaves.

He's right. Either I help her escape or the Messages get her. She's gone, either way.

Nia Silva is a profit opportunity. Or a risk, if she talks about the graffiti. And she's a dangerous distraction. How long did I blather about her to Mandi? And I didn't pay attention in chem today. Almost burned the lab down, watching out the window, wondering if she'd walk out of the woods and come back to school.

I can't let things slip. My father might notice even small changes. And that would be the end of everything. He'd take me to the Listening Room.

You sit in a padded hotel room for as long as it takes. There are speakers in the walls, the ceilings, the floor. The music never stops. And the Messages are custom-made just for you.

It's not uncomfortable, unless you count the sensation of being erased. The sheets are Egyptian cotton and the food is catered. I've heard Dad tell people it's like going to a spa. "It's refreshing. Restorative," he says. "It empties your mind of all its worries."

But there are side effects after you leave. Migraines. Intolerance of bright light. And for some, obsessive behavior. Touching a light switch twenty times. Staying up until dawn vacuuming.

The side effects fade over time. For most people.

Thinking about the Listening Room makes it easy. I think of the words again and this time they rush out.

Now I just have to hide my Message in music. I press open another panel and reach for the burlap bag between the wall studs. My laptop, hidden.

It takes just one special computer program, stolen by me. Two minutes later it's done. I have a CD with my instructions. I slide it into the hidden pocket inside my jacket. Tonight I'll play it. My brain will listen while I sleep.

I hear a thud. I freeze. Look and listen.

A sprinkler's hitting the shed every ten seconds as it rotates across the lawn. Frogs hum in the preserve behind the fence. All normal.

Another thud. No. Not normal. And now there's a scratching noise near the door. The doorknob is wiggling, just a little.

Someone's breaking in. Or they've got a key. I do a quick check: incriminating evidence in the cup, recorder on the chair, stash door wide open.

I slam the stash door shut, but the latch doesn't work. It pops open again. Another slam. It opens wider this time, showing even more of the goodies inside.

The Adirondack chairs. One of those beasts will keep the stash door shut. They're next to the door, but I risk it—check the knob, still wiggling—and throw my body against one. It barely moves. No way can I get it to the wall in time.

The doorknob goes still. Then the whole door shudders. Someone's throwing themselves against it.

I grab the cup. At least I can fix that. With one long swallow, I dispose of its contents. It's so strong it gives me a coughing fit. I stagger to my stash and lean against the door. Naughtiness concealed. If I stay where I am.

Hopefully whoever it is won't notice the recorder. Or make me move.

If I do, it's over.

The door crashes open. "Oscar! Oscar! Are you in here?"

Guess who.

I'm not caught. Just supremely annoyed.

"Shut the door. And stop yelling my name," I say. The words come out all shaky.

Sherman obeys. "I'm sorry. It's just—I'm—" He stops, panting.

He's wearing a huge backpack on his shoulders. Sweat has soaked through his polo shirt in patches: rings under his arms, and a big wet oval over his stomach.

"Taking your homework for a walk?" My hands are shaking. I pick up my cup like there's still something in it that's going to help.

"I waited for hours." He collapses into the chair I tried to move.

"Maybe you should go wait some more," I say. "For whatever."

Sherman grabs both arms of the chair. "I was waiting for *you*," he bellows.

"Shut up! You want to get us caught?"

"Why didn't you meet me?" Sherman pulls a wad of paper out of his pocket. Uncrumples it. "I did what you said. Enter the woods at the ninth hole of the golf course. Walk a quarter mile east—"

"Give me that." I grab the paper. "I *told* you not to write the directions down."

"But I can't remember anything."

"No kidding. What's today, Sherman?" I ball the paper up and shove it in my pocket. To be destroyed later.

"Today's Wednesday." He says it slow, like I'm the idiot.

"Right. Wednesday. Not Saturday."

"I know." He frowns. Blink. Blink. Then I see it coming. "You mean . . . I'm not supposed to leave tonight?"

"It's not happening tonight, Sherm. You leave *Saturday*. It was always Saturday."

He's breathing faster. He clutches at his sweaty polo shirt. "But I'm all packed. And I left a note."

"What kind of note? For who?"

My rules are very clear about good-byes. It's too risky—to them, but especially to me.

"It was to my mother." His lips are trembling. "And I don't care what you say."

"You think she loves you?" I laugh. "If she did, you wouldn't be stuck here."

"I'll miss her."

"Did you say anything about where you're going or how you'll get there?"

"I didn't say anything about you." His look is too superior, knowing. Like he's got something on me.

"You've really been waiting in the woods for two hours?"

"Maybe three. I wanted to get there in plenty of time."

"You're an unbelievable screwup, Sherman."

He nods. "I know."

"Why did I agree to take you on?"

"Because I gave you all my money."

"I can find other rich kids." Letting Sherman stay would be a liability. He might talk, even though I've fed him plenty of Messages telling him not to. But getting him out could be a bigger risk, since he's screwing up every single step. Maybe I just need to let the Messages take care of him—find a way to get him to the Listening Room. He'll never remember me after that. I've never tried to get a client erased before.

"Just call your guy and I'll get out of here," Sherman says. "I won't bug you anymore."

"I can't just call my guy." I don't even know Frank's phone number. "We have a system. There are certain protections. It takes days to get things set up."

It starts with a postcard. I write the time and date of pickup on the back. Nothing else. I mail it to a PO box fifty miles from here. Then Frank confirms the date. His business brings him to Candor almost every day, so he can leave me a note. We have three different hiding places.

Sherman moans. "What am I going to do? I can't go back. What if they already read the note?"

"Tell them it was a joke." But it won't work. If his parents found the note, they've probably already called my dad, and he's got the search parties out. Dad takes runaways very personally.

Search parties. I grab the lantern and turn it off, leaving the room pitch-black.

"What was that for?" Sherman's voice sounds even whinier in the dark.

"People might be looking for you." And I don't want them to find me.

"But—no! They'll send me to that place you told me about. Where they play the music until your ears bleed."

"That's an unusual side effect."

There's a sobbing sound. I relish it. He deserves to be afraid.

"You have to help me, Oscar. I paid you a lot of money."

If I had the cash, I'd throw it back in his face. I picture the green wad slapping him in the mouth. Nice.

But it's already squirreled away in one of my offshore accounts. "You didn't pay me for tonight," I tell him. "You paid me for Saturday. And I don't give freebies."

"Then . . . then I'll tell."

"You won't tell. You can't." My booster music would stop him. I've got plenty of safeguards in there: *Never tell anyone about Oscar's secret. Never tell anyone you know about the Messages.*

But what if? He's ignored everything else. Maybe those boosters aren't sinking in.

"I'll tell them everything," he says. "I'll say how you offered to help me escape, and I paid you all that money, and you showed me this shack—"

"Shed."

"Shed. And then you were mean to me, and then—"

It's too risky. I need him out, now. With him and Nia around, I've got too much to deal with.

"Take some supplies." I flick on the lantern and walk over to my stash. There's a box of chocolate protein bars. I give him half. He can live off his fat for the rest of the time.

Then I climb on the top of the potting table and reach into the rafters. There's a blanket hidden there. Sometimes I take the most interesting girls on a field trip to the golf course. The sixth hole has a nice, soft patch of grass that nobody can see from the road.

Sherman's already crammed a bar in his mouth by the time my feet hit the floor.

"Better make those last," I tell him. "You've got three days."

He stops chewing and his mouth drops open. There's a huge ball of chewed granola in there. "I thought I was leaving," he mumbles.

"I told you. I can't get you out. You'll have to hide until then."

Sherman clutches the blanket to his chest. Shakes his head.

"If they find you, they'll send you to the Listening Room."

"No. No. I don't want to change. I want to leave."

I flick off the lantern so it's dark again. The peanut smell of the bars fills the shed. "You have two choices. Hide or go home."

"I don't know where to hide." His voice is muffled, like he's got his mouth pressed into the blanket.

"There are places in the woods. An old orange grower's shack. And some platforms in the trees, from the days when people hunted here."

"I don't . . . *camp*. And who would make my dinner?"

"Maybe you'll find a private chef hiding under a palm tree," I tell him.

"*I* know!" His voice squeaks. "I could stay *here*!"

I picture people touring the shed. Finding blubbering, blathering Sherman playing with the silk flowers. "No," I tell him. "People will see you. We can't lock the shed for three days."

"Do you have any more of those bars?"

I hand over the rest. They were getting old anyway.

"See you Saturday." I go to the door and open it a crack. But he hasn't moved his fat butt.

"I'll go in a little bit," he says. "We could watch a movie or something."

I shut the door again. But I keep my hand on the knob. "You need to go before somebody finds you here. Besides, you'll want to find a place to sleep before the boars are out."

"Boars? Who are they?"

"Giant pissed-off wild pigs. They could lift you off the ground with their tusks."

"You're making that up." But he stands up, a lumbering mass in the dark.

"I'm not making it up. They'll chase you through half the woods." It's true. I know their favorite hangouts by now. And I never go near them after dark.

"Okay. Open the door." He's standing right next to me now. He smells sour, metallic. By Saturday he should be nice and ripe. Lucky Frank.

"Don't screw up," I tell him. "Saturday, nine o'clock, at the same place. If you're late, I'm not waiting."

"I'll be there." But he doesn't sound sure.

I'm not sure, either. Those boars can be nasty. But that would solve my Sherman problem, too.

I stand outside and watch him walk to the garden gate. It creaks a little when he opens it. He looks around nervously before stepping into the street. The gate slams shut behind him. Loud.

It makes me jump. But I don't hear anything: no hum of an electric car, no shouts of people looking for Sherman. Maybe he's got a head start. Maybe he'll make it through the next three days.

Whether he makes it out will be up to him.

And the boars.

chapter 7

THE LIBRARY CLOSES in five minutes. Can't make Dad suspicious.

I put my goodies back in their hiding spots and lock up.

Walking home, I keep my hand in my coat pocket. My fingers are wrapped around the CD. It'll fix everything. After one, maybe two nights. No more obsessing over flowery hair and long fingers. Fingers touching my lips, my skin, everything bare.

Dad's waiting on the porch. Guess Sherman's parents haven't found out their darling is missing. Dad would be at his office downtown fixing things—or trying to.

"Get lots of work done?" he asks.

"More than I planned." I wonder where Sherman will sleep tonight. Will he remember to listen to my Messages?

The woods don't have speakers. Dad's Messages don't reach the squirrels and the snakes. If Sherman goes nighty-night without his headphones, he'll lose it. Major withdrawal. Nobody's brain survives a whole night away.

I remember what happened to the Lockharts. They were one of the first families to move to Candor. And the first funeral.

They were driving to a funeral in Atlanta. But they never made it out of Florida. On their first—and last—night away, they checked into a motel by the interstate. And then their brains unraveled.

I wonder when they realized they'd forgotten their maintenance music. Who decided they could get it later, or maybe skip it altogether?

It was a fatal choice.

People in town think there was a car crash. But I saw the police pictures and news clippings hidden in Dad's desk.

It would have started with migraines and dizziness. Next come hallucinations. That could explain why Mrs. Lockhart hung herself. Or maybe that didn't happen until the psychosis set in. Which is probably when the kids attacked themselves with nail scissors and splintered DVDs.

At some point Mr. Lockhart left the room and jumped off an overpass.

Dad let himself into their house after the funeral. I was with him. There, on the front hall table, was a set of CDs. They were in a travel case.

Someone just forgot to bring them. And they all died.

That day, Dad cried. But it didn't change anything.

I warned Sherman. I told him what would happen without Messages. But he ignored all my other warnings.

"Get to bed." Dad stands up. The porch swing thumps against the windowsill. He forgets he's skinny, I think. He does everything with too much force.

I don't hug him good night. That stopped a long time ago.

I do all the things I'm supposed to. Floss. Wash behind my ears. Turn off the lights before eleven.

Sometimes it's nice to do what the Messages say. It's like sinking into a warm bath, eyes shut, arms floating, and letting the water cover my face. I don't have to breathe until someone tells me to.

There's just one last thing before I fall asleep.

The CD.

I'm not tired. It can wait. I'll just lie in bed and stare at the ceiling. Remind myself why she's a bad idea.

The dots are still on my ceiling. Random blobs of glow-in-the-dark paint that my mother put there. "It's our secret," she said. "Your father will never notice."

She was right. The dots are invisible in the day. And even if Dad came in my room at night, he wouldn't look up. He's strictly a forward-motion, eyes-on-the-prize guy. Goal oriented, he calls it.

He doesn't have time to look up or down or all around. Maybe that's why he never noticed my other invisible secrets.

When I couldn't sleep, Mom would lie on my bed with me, pointing at our dots. "I see a whale," she'd say. Or, "Look! It's Teddy Roosevelt!"

"I don't see that," I'd say, but hoping she'd find even more things. It was different every night.

She made me find things, too. At first it looked like a ceiling splattered with paint. But then lines would appear—a river, a school bus, a hippopotamus.

"I see it!" she'd say. "You found something spectacular."

After she left, I slept on my stomach. My side. But never on my back. I was afraid I'd see her dinosaur, her plate of cookies, the whale. Or worse, everything she showed me would be gone.

Tonight I look. But there's nothing—just dots. Mom used to call it a ceiling of infinite possibilities. Now I just don't believe in it. I was right not to look all those years.

To survive, I have to be heads-down. Like Dad. One goal. One direction.

I slide my fingers over the music player's buttons. I feel strong enough to hit play now and start erasing the potential of Nia.

The music is classical piano, soothing, perfect for bedtime. Six hours from now, things will be back to normal. But my eyes won't close and my legs want to run. I give up on lying down. My feet take me to the window over my desk—the one I saw her through.

The blinds are closed. I flick them open.

And jump back. Someone's staring in at me. I try to swear, but my brain won't let it happen. My mouth is too busy hanging open like a fish.

But then I see he's black and white. A man on paper.

Someone taped a drawing to my window.

I slide it open.

Loud sirens sound from the hallway. "Intruder alert! Intruder alert!"

The house alarm. Dad arms it every night, just in case someone comes from the outside and breaks his perfect bubble. If the county would let him, he'd put a big gate around the entire town to keep the wrong people out and the right people in.

Someone bangs on my door. "Safety word!" Dad barks.

"Hot dog!" I shout. Our old just-in-case word. "But Dad—"

"Stay there and lock your door!"

I should follow him down the hall and tell him it's all right—that there's nobody dangerous in the house.

I pull the paper off the glass and shut the window. Lock my door.

It's not a man—it's a kid my age. His eyes are wide—scared? Or shocked? But his lips are set and tense. He holds up one finger to his mouth. A warning to be quiet.

It's good. Really good.

A note is on the bottom: *Thanks for the tunes.*

As if I needed her to tell me she made this.

The alarm shuts off. I can hear the piano music again. It's too loud. I can't stand it another second and I shut it off.

There's only the regular house music left: the closest to silence it gets here. Dad knocks on the door. "Open up."

My hand is on the knob when I feel the paper between my fingers. I ball it up and stick it under my pillow, then I let him in.

"Everything okay?" I throw in a yawn for effect.

Dad shakes his head. "Alarms don't go off by themselves. First graffiti. Now attempted break-ins."

"Candor is our safe haven." The Message bubbles over my lips, easy, the perfect thing to say.

"That's right, son." Dad claps a heavy hand on my shoulder. "I'll make sure of it."

I flinch, not meaning to—just surprised he touched me.

He jerks away like I'm a hot stove. Danger. Don't touch the child. "Get some sleep."

I lie down. The paper crinkles under the pillow. I wait five minutes, just in case.

Then I pull it out. Hold it up high, so it's outlined by glowing blobs. In the dark I can see who it is.

She drew me. But not who I see in the mirror. Nia saw the Oscar I keep hidden. And she put him on paper.

Nobody sees the real me. Not since I stopped looking for pictures on my ceiling.

Finally I'm sleepy. I pull up my usual playlist. Hit play.

Nia's making it hard to want to forget her. I should hate her for it.

But I crumple the drawing again. Hold the ball tight against my chest.

I stay on my back when I close my eyes. Even with my eyes shut, I see dots and lines and glowing giraffes. And a girl, drawing.

Seeing the lines between my dots.

chapter 8

NIA IS ALL I can think about.

But that doesn't mean I have to *act* stupid.

I'll be the same person I was before she skateboarded down my sidewalk. Charming, studious, obedient Oscar Banks.

Safe Oscar Banks.

So I serve Dad's rye toast with a smile. Raise my hand in every class. The chess club gets the pleasure of my company at lunch.

And when the president of the school's newest club asks for my help, I say yes. That's the kind of thing Oscar Banks does. He's an exceptional person.

Especially when he's going out with the president of that club. Good Oscar wants to make Mandi Able happy. Which means taking orders from a blonde with a clipboard.

"Come to the four-way stop by the flagpole after last period," she tells me. "TAG will supply the chalk. Don't be late. I mean, please."

TAG. I think she was babbling about it yesterday. Probably I should act like I know what she's talking about.

But she knows me too well. "Remember TAG? Teens Against Graffiti? I told you all about it yesterday after study group." She gives me a blue-eyed laser stare. "It's my top priority. This town is facing a crisis."

"Right. Graffiti crisis. How could I forget?"

"And today we're putting pride Messages on our sidewalks," she says. Like she's told me this part before, too. Not that I remember. That might have been when I was wondering what it looks like when a girl skateboards naked. What's the better view? Front or back?

Whoops. There I go again.

Pull it together, Oscar.

"You're writing on the sidewalks?" I ask.

"I have eighty catchy phrases right here." She taps on her clipboard.

It's too funny to be real. "Isn't that graffiti?"

She pulls the clipboard tight to her chest, which is regrettably shrouded in a loose shirt. "It's a statement. It's anti-graffiti."

"I guess if we cover the sidewalks, there's no room for graffiti," I tease.

But she takes me seriously. Acts like I just came up with the cure for cancer. "Good point, Oscar! I never thought of that. We'll need to think about how we can protect the lamp poles, too."

She hurries off without a good-bye, or even a reminder to be there.

But I will be there. Because I'm being good. Or at least I'm trying.

When I get to the intersection after school, TAG's fearless leader is waiting for me. "You're late," Mandi says.

"School ended fifteen minutes ago."

She sweeps her hand around the intersection. Every sidewalk square has a kid working on it. "Some people made this a priority."

Sometimes even the Messages can't stop the real Mandi from popping out. "I love it when you're mean," I tell her.

"I'm not mean! Always be kind to others!" Her eyes are wide and hurt. I feel a little bad for tweaking her.

"Just kidding. You're not mean." Not nearly often enough.

"We're doing twenty squares in each direction. Let's find one for you. Come." She starts walking. I follow.

We pass kids writing things on their assigned patches of concrete. *PUT DOWN THE PAINT AND PICK UP A BOOK!* And *UGLY PEOPLE MAKE UGLY GRAFFITI!*

Catchy. If Dad ever needs someone to write Messages, he should put Mandi on the payroll.

Every square is taken. "There must be a blank area somewhere." Mandi shades her eyes and looks around.

If I leave now, I'll have the whole afternoon free. Time to think about Nia. To look for her. To . . . no. I'm not going to do that.

"I can just go to the end," I tell her, pointing down one sidewalk.

Then I see the square at the end. It's different from the rest. Swirling colors and black jagged lettering, like real graffiti. Nia is kneeling next to it.

There's no escape.

My heart double-times it. I take a deep breath. Got to stay in control.

"Maybe I don't need you," Mandi says. She's still looking around. I don't think she's noticed Nia's square.

"Let me help."

"It's symmetrical. We can't just add on to the end. You can go."

Now is my chance to get away. To do the smart thing.

But I don't. I look straight into my girlfriend's eyes and say, "I'll figure out some way to help you."

"That's sweet, even if it's unnecessary." She gives me a twinkly little smile. Then a kid asks her for help on his square.

I am dismissed.

My feet take me to Nia faster than they should.

She looks up from her drawing. "You again?"

"Our town is facing a crisis," I tell her. "A graffiti crisis."

"You'd know all about that, Picasso."

"Quiet," I whisper. Look around. Is there anyone listening? "Don't—"

"I won't." She waves her hand dismissively, still holding chalk.

I sit on the grass next to her. Not too close. "I like your square."

"Thanks. Better get started on yours." Nia pushes the box of chalk toward me. "If you think you can handle the competition."

It's not the competition I'm worried about. It's the company. Maybe I should go.

But it's possible to be good around her. Has to be.

I'll prove it.

"I can handle anything you dish out." I pick out a white piece.

The stick is powdery and fragile. It's been years since I touched chalk. Did we even bring some when we moved? I can't remember.

Nia is watching me. "Are you going to smoke it or draw with it?"

"Watch the master at work." I scrape the white stick over the sidewalk. It barely leaves a mark.

"That was pathetic."

"I'm out of practice."

"You have to press harder," she says, putting her hand over mine. Her fingers feel surprisingly strong.

Together we make a thick, wobbly line. Then her fingers are gone, fast. Pushed away by Messages, I bet. They're pulsing in my brain. Warning me.

Respectful space in every place.

Avoid physical contact.

"It's a worm." I put my hands on my cheeks in mock horror. "A really ugly one. You ruined my square."

"You needed my help, Picasso."

"See all the other squares? No worms."

"Now the worm gets an apple." Before I can stop her, she sketches one.

"Stay in your own square." But I put my foot in the corner of hers.

Is it her? Or the chalk? I want to play. I want to remember when that was okay. Like I'm six again.

"My square." She jabs at my shoe with her chalk. It leaves a green smudge.

"Hey, freshly polished!" I pull my shoe back.

"In that case . . ." She leaves another streak of green on my shoes.

I retaliate with a long white mark through the bottom of her square. A straight line over all her thick, curling shapes.

"You violated the masterpiece!" she shrieks.

I feel kids staring. Wondering. But when I look up, their eyes are pointed at their piece of sidewalk. Always do your best.

Another good time to leave.

But I stay. Again. Not doing the smart thing. When I'm around this girl, I lose my brain. I know it and I still can't help myself.

Nia grabs the chalk from my hand and pounces on my square. She fills it with white and green, laughing, hair swinging, arms smeared with color. I bet she doesn't care who's watching. Doesn't worry about what they think.

She's beautiful. And dangerous.

When she's done there's no hint of sidewalk left. The square is entirely covered in color. "Handle that." She flings the chalk at me.

I catch it.

Her smile looks tasty and right. I don't want it to go away. But what can I do? How do I keep up with her? Can I do it and stay safe?

"You're a chalk criminal," I tell her.

She holds up both hands, high in the air. "Guilty as charged."

I want to touch her again. Even if it's against the rules. *Respectful space in every place.*

Screw the Message.

Still, I check for Mandi first. Is she around? No.

I get to play some more.

"Give me your hand," I order.

She holds out one fist. I uncurl her fingers and turn them so the palm is facing up. Then I rub the chalk on her skin. Color each finger, taking my time.

Once she tries to jerk away. "Wait," I tell her. And she listens. Watches my hand color hers.

When her palm and fingers are entirely green, I stop. Press her hand on the pavement. "Fingerprints," I tell her.

"Amateur. It's done like this." She rolls each finger over the chalk. A pro. Not surprising, given her history.

"Perfect. Now everyone knows who ruined my square," I tease.

And then Mandi is there. How long was she watching?

Her mouth is pulled tight. She points at our squares. "What's that?"

"It's art," Nia says. "Heard of it?"

"But art is useless." Mandi crosses her arms.

"You can't be serious." Nia stands up. She towers over Mandi.

"It gets your attention," I say. "So then you read the other stuff."

Mandi was staring at Nia. But now she's looking at the sidewalk. "Nobody will miss this."

"Thank you." Nia takes a little bow.

Then Mandi looks back up at her. "It's not like the others."

"Which is kind of the point," Nia says.

"It's really okay," I tell Mandi.

"Conformity is beauty." Mandi lets out a single shuddering sob. Then she walks away, toward the closest building.

"You blew her circuits," Nia says.

Am I supposed to follow her? Apologize? Console her?

I don't know the answer, so I stay where I want to be. Next to Nia.

Mandi is headed for the bushes. To hide? Or shred them with her perfectly straight teeth in a fit of rage? She twists the spigot behind the bushes. Grabs the hose that's attached.

"Bad news for the worms," I say.

"No. I won't let her." Nia tosses her hair. Tendrils stick to her cheeks.

"It's not a big deal. It's just chalk." I don't want a scene. Especially one I'm in the middle of.

She turns a fierce stare at me. "Art is never *just* chalk."

Tell it to the hose. But I don't argue. Instead I look at our squares and try to memorize them. Truth is, I don't want them gone, either.

Mandi is moving fast, dragging the hose behind her. Water is shooting from the nozzle. But then she stops about fifteen feet away. The hose is too short.

She tries raising it. Points it at us. But the water doesn't come close.

Nia laughs. "Awesome."

Mandi looks at the hose. Looks at Nia's sidewalk. Drops the hose. She doesn't even bother to turn it off. It squirms in the grass, spewing water.

"Yes!" Nia pumps her fist in the air.

"She never gives up that easily," I tell her.

Mandi walks to the green metal box that's poking out from under an oak tree's mulch. It's helpfully labeled. Easy to tell what's inside.

She wouldn't. It would mess with her whole project.

"Stop! You'll ruin them all," I call out.

She shakes her head. No. No, I will not listen. Or no, I don't care. I'm not sure what she means. But I'm certain of what she's going to do.

We are all about to get very wet.

The box clangs open. No need for locks in Candor. Nobody touches things they shouldn't—except in an emergency.

And for Mandi, this must be an emergency.

"What's she doing?" Nia asks.

A low hiss sounds by our feet. Like a snake. A big one.

"Sprinklers. Run!" I turn tail and head for dry ground.

But when I look back, Nia's not with me.

The sprinklers are on full blast. Everyone's chalk is dissolving, running in muddy streams to the storm sewers. Except Nia's—at least, except a small piece of hers.

She has her feet planted on the sidewalk. Long legs spread wide. One black boot on her square. The other on mine. Her smile is fierce.

"Handle this!" she yells. Then she holds one hand out to me. Come.

I see Mandi a block away, surrounded by her faithful. Staying dry. But watching.

There's no way I can do what I want. Go to Nia. Jump in the sprinklers. Ignore all the eyes staring at us.

But I feel like I owe her an explanation. I edge closer, so I'm just getting sprayed on my legs. "I have homework," I shout. "I should go."

She holds up her other hand. The one I colored. It's still green.

When I don't move, she makes a fist and jams it in her pocket.

"Have fun being normal," she says.

"I always do," I lie.

I leave her to get soaked. I leave our art to get dissolved. When does the water stop? How does she get home, sopping wet?

I don't know, because I leave the whole mess behind.

Then I take Mandi out for ice cream.

It's the safe thing to do.

chapter 9

SATURDAY STARTS LIKE it's supposed to. I get the paper. Toast four slices of rye. Brew coffee.

But nothing feels normal. Sherman was missing from school for the rest of the week. Either he's hiding, waiting for tonight, or caught. Not knowing is killing me.

I look for him everywhere I go: school, the grocery store. But all I find is Nia. Teasing eyes. Curving lips. I hurry away before I do something else stupid. She doesn't follow.

When Dad shows at the table, he grabs a thermos from the cabinet, fills it with coffee, and wraps his toast in a paper towel. "Go get the tackle box," he says. "And the poles."

"Fishing?" We never go fishing. Not anymore.

I remember when I would have been excited. Now it's just making me nervous. Everything that's different is making me nervous, since Sherman left. It could be the beginning of the end. A sign that I'm caught.

He looks at his watch. "Better hurry."

"But I don't know where the tackle box—"

"Garage, left of the door. Third shelf from the bottom, behind the hibiscus fertilizer."

A Message drip-drops on my brain. *Always obey your parents.*

Asking questions will only make him suspicious. That's not the kind of thing good Candor kids do. So I go to the garage.

The box is right where he said it would be. It's rusty. Fingerprints make polka dots in the thick dust on top. One of the latches is missing.

It's not how it used to be. Not even close.

The tackle box was my grandfather's. He gave it to Dad. Then Dad gave it to Winston for his tenth birthday. I was four. I wanted that box. It was smooth and red and shiny. Like a fire truck. But my brother wouldn't let me touch it. "You won't keep it nice," he said.

"I will, I promise," I told Winston. He didn't believe me. I guess he was right. But it doesn't matter. He's not alive to see it.

I'm not even supposed to remember he existed.

The thermometer on Dad's rearview mirror reads 90, and it's only 8:45 A.M. "Great fishing weather," I say.

He nods. Either he's ignoring my attitude or he doesn't believe it's real.

I try again. "Maybe it's too hot. We could go tomorrow." Or never.

Dad gives a quick shake of this head. "Things are set for today."

What things? I want to ask. But I'm not supposed to be afraid of my father. He's my idol in my pretend life.

So I stay quiet. Besides, what else can I do? Run away screaming?

We park a block away from the pond. "Don't want to block the view," Dad says.

The pond is in the middle of downtown Candor, with cafés and shops across the street from it. They made the pond when Dad built the town. Scooped out dirt to fill people's lots. Filled it with water.

Insert fish. Instant nature.

Broad cement steps down to the water. There are rocking chairs on each step, with green umbrellas on stands. People are already using them this morning.

"Chip. Phyllis." Dad nods at some people in the chairs. I look more closely. All but one of the rocking people work at Town Hall. We're surrounded.

They give me big smiles but look away fast. The way you'd react if you saw a celebrity.

"Did you make them sit here?" I ask.

Dad sets the tackle box in the shade and flips the lid up. "It's early. I didn't want the pond looking lonely."

"For who?"

He pulls out a frog lure and attaches it to his line. Makes the first cast of the day. It's perfect: long and straight. Lands with barely a splash.

Finally he speaks. "Thought I told you. Big bus coming in today. Brits."

He paid people to ride their bikes or walk their dogs past the models, in the early days. When it was just him and me and Mom living here.

Maybe he's telling me the truth. Or maybe not.

"We don't need the business, do we?" The waiting list is years long. Why does he care about a bus full of sunburned British tourists?

"No such thing as too much business."

I don't know why I asked. He always says that. It's like he thinks the waiting list is a savings account.

Maybe that really is why I'm here: I'm a prop. It must look nice. Father and son, fishing together. Ah, Candor. Home of the happy family. Or in our case, what's left of it.

Or maybe it's a trap.

We used to go fishing for fun. When I was little, Mom and Dad rented a cabin in Wisconsin. Every morning we took the rowboat out. I baited the hook. Winston cast the line. Dad reeled them in. He liked to say we caught dinner before breakfast.

"Remember Mom's fishcakes?" I ask. The spicy-sweet taste is on my tongue. She put cinnamon in them, and cayenne pepper. They were delicious.

Dad gives me a sharp look. I've been stupid. "The past is behind us."

It's what he always says when I bring up things like that. And I know what to say back. It slides out so easily. "We must focus on the future."

"Good man." Dad's smile looks satisfied. I feel a little safer.

But it's not easy to stuff away memories. I remember how the orange life vests pressed against our chins. They smelled like wet dirt. Dad always checked the buckles before he untied the boat.

"Hot today," Dad says. "They'll be deep."

"This is nice," I say. Because it kind of is. If I forget it's just for show. Pretend Sherman and Nia and orange graffiti never happened. There's nothing to be afraid of, if that were true.

"People want something when they see someone else using it. Remember that." Dad casts his line. It goes so far, it looks like it's halfway across the pond.

"Everybody wants to be part of the crowd," I say. Another one of his business theories.

"You're going to be smarter than your old man before we know it," he says. "I taught you well." More than he knows. I learned how to make the Messages by spying on him. Reading manuals, hacking into his computer, listening on the phone. He never bothered to protect things well. He thought the Messages made sure I wasn't curious.

He's never understood that I'm different from him. We don't want all the same things.

Dad gives my line a tug. "It's loose."

I whirl the reel and the line slowly shortens.

"Kid tried to run away the other night," he says.

My hand freezes. I feel the presence of all his loyal workers around me.

"Who was it?" I try to sound shocked. And worried.

"Sherman Golub." His eyes slide over my face. I stare out at the pond.

"Is he gone?" I ask.

Dad snorts. "Found him ten feet into the woods, behind his own house. He didn't really want to leave. Candor is his home."

Guess I won't have to sneak out tonight for our appointment.

Maybe I should feel sorry. He was my client. He paid me to get him out. And that didn't happen. I got money for nothing.

But I'm not sorry. I'm pissed. And scared.

Sherman knows things. Without my booster music, he might forget those things are a secret. All it will take is the right question.

"Is he okay?" I ask.

I hope they skipped the questions and took him straight to the Listening Room. I hope they stuffed him with so many Messages, there isn't room for anything else. If I'm lucky he's forgotten all about me.

"The boy needed some family time. He'll be back to school on Monday."

Does family time mean the Listening Room—good for me, bad for Sherman? Or does it mean snuggling with Mommy and telling her all my secrets?

Dad casts his line out again, straight and strong. The lure drops without a sound. It's like the water just opened up and swallowed.

My cast stops short, with a splash. So much for casual and in control. I'm probably chasing the fish straight to Dad's hook.

I thought I'd feel better when I knew what happened to Sherman. But now there are fewer questions, more fear.

I feel like I'm supposed to say something. Should I be happy he'll be back? Or am I not supposed to care? For once the Messages are silent—just when I need them.

"You ever talk with the Golub boy?" Dad asks.

"Just . . . derivatives. Math stuff." Like the hefty chunk of change he deposited in my offshore account.

No refunds. No matter what.

"Things could have been different." Dad turns his head and looks at me. His hand keeps turning the reel.

Am I supposed to apologize? Agree? I wait for a Message to tell me what to do.

"You're a leader. A boy like that would follow your example. He'd do what you told him he should," Dad says.

A laugh fills my mouth. I press my lips shut to keep it silent.

"No need to be modest. We both know you're my clone." Dad chuckles and reaches his hand up toward my head. But when I meet his eyes, his arm drops to his side.

I try to transform the hysterical laughter inside into a proud smile. My lips tremble with the effort. "I wish I could help."

Other than shutting down my highly profitable, intensely annoying-to-my-father business. That won't happen.

"You will help." His voice is so certain. "There's another new one. Antonia Silva. She's your age."

Nia. I feel a drop of sweat roll down my spine. "The name is kind of familiar."

Did someone tell him about the chalk and the sidewalks? Is this another test?

"Girl's not adjusting well. Her parents are worried. They came by my office yesterday when they heard about the Golub boy."

I "mm-hmm" and hold my hand over my eyes to look out at the pond. Like I can see fish leaping in the distance.

"I told them you'd help."

I look at him. He's still watching me. I keep my face blank. "Um. How?"

"You're her new best friend. Wherever you go, she goes. You'll keep her straight."

The best thing for him would be to keep Nia far away from me. It would be the best thing for me, too.

"I think Mandi might be upset," I tell him. "She's my girl-friend."

"Give her a few days," he says. "She'll get over it."

I think about the day I found Nia drawing in the park, when Mandi found us. She didn't seem so happy then. Things haven't been exactly cozy between us since the sidewalk thing, either.

I love this idea. And hate it. Safer to stick with the hating part. "I have midterms coming up."

"Find a way to make it work."

"And college applications. Plus all my chores. I wouldn't want to stop doing my chores. It's important to help one's parents." I get a perverse pleasure of spitting out his Messages when it's inconvenient for him.

But it rolls off him. "This girl needs a good example. And it's go-ing to be you." He casts his line out again, confident and smooth.

Who's going to be my good example? Who's going to show me how to ignore how she makes me feel? How I want to do stupid, dangerous things when it comes to her?

Anger washes over me. That would have been Winston's job.

But he screwed up. Everyone knows safety comes first. Even people who aren't brainwashed.

I should be happy. I'm safe, at least for today. Sherman didn't spill. Dad thinks I'm his adoring protégé.

I sigh. Shrug my shoulders. "I guess I can."

"Just don't get attached," he says. "Everyone leaves eventually."

He says it all the time. But he forgets: I've never left. Don't I count? Even if I'm the only one?

Winston was gone first. He snapped his neck, flipping off the diving board at my tenth birthday party. Dad had told him not to. But he did it anyway. Winston was never good at listening.

They wouldn't let me look. I stood by the cupcakes, my back to the pool. Chocolate frosting, with sugar cowboy hats, melting in the sun. Secretly I'd thought they looked babyish. I stuck my finger in one and licked it.

It tasted like sand.

The paramedics rushed him away with a siren and blinking lights. They acted like it was an emergency. Brought him to the hospital. But I heard people talking at the wake. Winston died before they pulled him from the water.

That was before Candor. Mom didn't leave until after we moved here. She only stayed a few months.

Don't go looking for me. She wrote it on the back of a grocery store receipt. I found it under my pillow.

She didn't write *I'll miss you.* Or *Sorry to be doing this.*

But I've never left. I've always been the good son. And now I'm the only one.

Dad's all I've got, too. He's the only one I trust. I don't like what he does. But he's easy to predict.

"You don't have to worry about me," I tell him.

"I never do." He gives me a smile. And for a second I feel like I am good. I am exactly who my father wants me to be. Sometimes I want that.

"I'll invite her over for flash cards," I say. "And sit with her at lunch."

"Good start." Then his line jerks. "A bite!" He starts reeling.

It's eighteen or nineteen inches, with beautiful gray-green scales. "You got a big one," I say.

"Even the fish listen to me." He grins and holds the line up high.

I watch the gills flap in and out. My stomach clenches. I think, for a second, that I'm going to puke.

"What a beaut." He turns around and waves. Unbelievable. There's the tour bus, creeping past us. Some of the tourists cheer.

It was for real. This isn't a trap. I'm just a prop for the tour bus.

I reach for the fish. "It can't breathe."

"I'm done anyway." He hands me the pole and heads for the bus.

I slide the hook out of the fish's lip. Then I kneel and set the fish in the water. It stays in place. Waves its tail once, twice.

"Welcome to Candor!" I can hear Dad from here. He'll climb on the bus next. Invite people to stay a bit. Get some cold water in our stunning model homes.

The fish twists its whole body.

"Go," I whisper.

One more flex of its tail and it's gone.

It's not impossible to escape my father. It just takes a little help.

chapter 10

SHE SHOWS UP that night.

The doorbell rings when I'm scraping the pan clean of burned fish bits. Dad checks his watch. "She's late. Work on that with her."

"With who?" I ask. But he's already gone to the front hall.

At first I think it must be an outsider. Saturday is family night in Candor. Some people go bowling. Others head to a G-rated movie. For most families, it's just another night of brainwashed bliss, never fighting or wanting to be somewhere else. For me and Dad, it's the only time we sit in the same room without a meal involved.

All the magic happens at the dining room table. Dad works on his laptop. I sit across the table from him. Either I do my homework or write a scholarship essay.

We don't talk; it's family night, not miracle night. But sometimes Dad gets crazy and makes hot-air popcorn. No salt, no butter, but it beats dry toast.

"Oscar, you've got a visitor," Dad says.

I look over my shoulder. There's Nia, dressed in a gauzy white shirt and tiny khaki shorts. My breathing goes unsteady.

"I know you just love homework." She drops a huge book bag on the floor. "So I brought you mine."

Dad chuckles and shakes his head. "Now, Antonia. Oscar can't do your homework for you."

She fixes him with a stare. "Everyone has a price."

"You're funny, very funny." He pats her on the head like a dog. She ducks the second pat and steps away from him.

I want her here. Dad wants her here. But the Messages are pushing in. *Saturday night is family night. Save your weekends for family time. Make your family a priority.*

Can't fight all of them all of the time. My brain forces out the words. "Why now? It's family night."

Something flickers across Nia's face. Whether it's hurt or amusement, I can't tell.

I clench my hands into fists and force them back. *I control the Messages.*

"Everyone in Candor is our extended family." Dad lifts his hand as if to pat her head again, then thinks twice. He jams his hand in his pocket instead. "And she needs some focused studying time."

Nia lets out a big sigh. "No Scrabble for me tonight."

I can't tell if she's sad or not. My eyes drift down to the white gauze of her shirt. Not as see-through as you'd imagine. Or hope.

"Go get your schoolbooks," Dad says. "I'll get Nia set up in the dining room."

This wasn't exactly what I had in mind for Nia. Doing homework with my father watching isn't going to lead to anything entertaining. But it's better than a regular Saturday night. So I grab my calc and chem books and hurry back downstairs.

When I get there, Dad's standing at the front door. He's holding a small green paper bag with brown handles. The Candor crest is on the side.

"I have a delivery to make," he says.

Only one thing goes in those bags: custom booster music. Dad never lets anyone else deliver them. He likes to jaw with the parents for a while when he drops them off. Then they play the music together. I think he likes to watch kids change, right in front of him.

He could be gone for hours.

Still, it must be pretty urgent to interrupt family night. I wonder if it's Sherman. But what do I care? He just gave me a solo Saturday night with Nia.

It's terrifying. And I can't wait.

"See you later," I say.

"Be good, son," he says. His usual good-bye.

Nia's got a book open on the table. She's highlighting it yellow. It makes her look like a Candor girl chasing a perfect GPA. For a second, she reminds me of Mandi.

Then she shows me the book with a twinkly smile. "Look. My new masterpiece."

There's a yellow checkerboard pattern across the two pages. I don't think it has anything to do with the exciting chapter about the nature of savanna climates.

"Never destroy school property," I say. Or my brain says. Another Message, flying out of my mouth.

Her smile fades. She sets the book down and flips the page. "You missed a good time in the sprinklers," she says.

An image of her dancing naked in the water pops in my head. But even my imagination refuses to put me there next to her.

"You're mad." I worried that she would be. Then I told myself I shouldn't care.

But I do.

"Not mad, not surprised," she says.

"Fine. Sorry. I just had to go."

"I stayed there for an hour," she says. "The sprinklers never turned off."

A fresh swell of guilt fills my gut. I could have switched the sprinklers off, at least. Or told Mandi to do it.

"But then I peeked under my boot. It was all gone. Without me even knowing, it washed away." She streaks her highlighter in a new pattern on the book.

I don't know what to say. I sit in the chair across from her. Pick up her earth-science book. It's the easiest science course Candor offers.

"They're making me repeat a bunch of stuff," she says. "I pretty much missed the last two years of high school."

"Where were you?" Although I pretty much know.

"Places you've never been." She tries to smile, like it's a joke. But her lips tremble. She stares at the table.

"I could help you catch up," I offer.

"You'd have to keep me awake first." Her smile makes my mouth go dry.

"I . . . could try." Weak, Oscar. Weak.

"Was tonight your idea?" she asks. "Did you make your father do this?"

"No. But he told me we have to hang out." Great. Make her think you don't want to be with her, Oscar. Can I say anything right tonight?

Her eyebrows flick up and down. "So you're the positive influence my mother was talking about."

"That's me. Pretty ironic, huh?"

She shrugs. "Not really. Seems like you're pretty good at being good."

"I'm only good when it's useful." I toss the book on the floor. "Screw this."

"Okay, then." She slaps her book shut and leans back in the chair. Crosses her arms and stares at me.

"What?"

"What next, rebel boy?"

"Um." I can think of a few things I've done with plenty of girls. But none of them seem right with her. I don't know where to start.

"How long until he's back?" she asks.

"Hours, if we're lucky." Twenty minutes if we're not.

"Then let's start with the grand tour." She slides her palm over the glossy table. Her fingers leave streaks. "I want to see opulence."

"Big word. I bet you're good at Scrabble."

"Dad's an English professor. There's too much pressure. When I was six, I ate the X tile." She mimes popping something in her mouth and swallowing.

"I ate the yellow guy from Candyland in kindergarten," I tell her. I'd forgotten until now. "Well, half of him. Just the head, really."

She laughs. A real laugh. It makes me think of strawberries and bubbles.

We start in the laundry room. I show her the panel that controls all the lights and music in the house. The digital readout says Dad's Music Mix 9 is playing. Your basic reinforcement Messages. "Music. Minimum volume," I say.

The house goes quiet—almost. You can barely hear the music. It's possible to ignore it, if you want. Though your subconscious will keep listening.

Nia rolls her head back and closes her eyes. Her shoulders sag. "Thank you. I'm so sick of music, all the time."

"Are you listening to my music?"

She makes a face. "Yeah. My parents took all my good music away. So I'm stuck with yours."

"Good. Keep listening."

The jazz is decent. "You have good taste, even if you are a positive influence."

I show her the oven that refrigerates food until it's ready to cook. The pantry with shelves that light up when a box gets too light—time to replace it. Upstairs, we stop by the home theater with the massage chairs.

"Where's your room?" she asks.

"It's not exciting." But she insists, so I show her. White walls. Twin bed. A desk with plenty of room for thick textbooks.

She looks for a minute. "It's basic." Her voice is too nice, like she feels sorry for me.

"It used to be great," I tell her. "There were these model train tracks hanging from the ceiling, and a bed shaped like a caboose."

"What happened?"

"I grew up." And people weren't touring our house anymore.

She walks over to my desk. "It's so empty."

"It doesn't matter." The shed is my real hideout now.

"I could paint something for you. Or draw something on the wall," she says.

"That's, um, nice of you," I say. Surprised, I guess. And wondering what my father would do if a piece of art showed up in our house.

"Or not." She rolls her eyes.

But then she spots it. A corner of paper showing below the Yale calendar on my wall. Her drawing, where my dad would never notice.

"You kept it." She yanks down the calendar. "You liked it."

"You're a crazy stalker," I tell her.

"Crazy *artist* stalker." She's got a smile on her face that I bet tastes like champagne.

I pin the calendar back up. "Come on. My dad won't be gone forever."

We finish the tour in Dad's bathroom. It's bigger than our kitchen back in Chicago, with countertops ripped from some mountain in Brazil. Nia pushes the button to turn on the shower. We watch all thirty jets pulse water against the tiny Italian tiles.

The noise fills my head. Pushes everything else out. Whatever I say belongs to me. I can be the guy with the orange paint can.

"It's made for two people," I tell her. "I could show you."

She gives me a shove. "You talk to your girlfriend that way?"

"She never notices. We're not . . . like that."

"Show me the backyard." Nia pushes past me. Before I know it, she's at the sliding-glass doors at the back of the house.

The backyard is the one place I don't want to be with her. Or anyone.

"Maybe we should study," I shout.

But she's already gone outside.

chapter 11

SHE'S STARING AT the pool when I catch up. "Why did you waste my time with the pervy shower? It's amazing out here."

I swallow. The spit barely slides down.

Nia looks up at the porch ceiling. "Hey, house. Turn some lights on." Nothing happens.

"Lighting," I say. "Backyard. Mid-level ambience. Spots on the trees."

Her eyes get huge as the lights brighten and fade to their new settings. "It's like you have a movie set in your backyard."

Our pool is top-of-the-line. There are two waterfalls, and an island in the middle with a built-in cooler. It's exactly what you would expect Campbell Banks to have in his backyard. Unless you knew his family history. But nobody knows that here. Nobody but him. And me.

"Are these real?" Nia skips over to the boulders around the edge of the water. I follow. Slowly.

"They're fake." I run my finger over the bumpy, cool surface. "It took three men a month to sculpt them."

She sits on the edge of the water and unlaces her ripped black sneakers. Then she slides her feet in the water, toes pointed. "You must swim here every day."

"We never use it." I can see the red ambulance lights, bouncing off another pool's water. I take one step back. Then another.

"Liar!" She flips her foot back and water spots my shirt.

"Careful!" I jump back another step. But I still don't feel safe.

"Do you fill it with acid?" She laughs.

"We aren't big swimmers." My voice cracks, and I have to look away. I squeeze my eyes shut. Don't cry. Don't think about it.

It helps until I open my eyes and see the brick patio. Old Chicago bricks, from our last place. I never understood why Mom made Dad bring them here.

Dad cried the day they were delivered. That was the day he started playing the Messages.

"What's wrong?" Her voice is gentle.

I bite the inside of my cheek. "Let's talk over here." I walk over and perch on the edge of a wicker lounge chair. But she doesn't move.

"You want to talk?" she says. "Then come put your feet in."

She stirs the water with her feet. Flashes of black-painted toenails. Pale skin, almost white under the water.

I shake my head.

"Sit," she says. "That's all."

So I sit next to her. I sit so close, our hips touch.

"My name isn't Mandi." She edges away.

"You want me to sit or not?" I meant to sound tough. But my voice cracks.

She comes closer. "Put your feet in."

"I don't swim."

Then she squeezes my hand tight, just once, and lets go. "I'll keep you safe."

I'm nervous. So nervous I barely notice the five seconds of hand-holding.

The water doesn't own me. Nothing will happen. I can take care of myself.

I kick off my sandals. Slide my feet into the pool. It's warm. Soft. My muscles relax, just a little. "I never knew it was heated."

"It's nice," she says. "Dad filled my pool with a hose, when I was little. We got it for five bucks at the grocery store."

I risk a kick. Watch the water fly off my toes.

"So you like my drawing?" she asks. Shy, for once.

"It's amazing." I wish I could make something from nothing. But all I do is work the system. I take what's been dealt and do my best.

"I can teach you," she says.

"Don't bother." It's not supposed to sound mean.

But she bites her lip and looks away.

I feel like I owe her an explanation. "My mother tried, for years. But my brother was the artistic one."

"You have a brother? Where do you keep him, under a rock?" She thumps one of the boulders. It makes a hollow thud.

"I don't have a brother. Not anymore." Or ever, as far as anyone in Candor knows. I pull one foot out of the water and hug my knee close. I don't know why I told her that.

"Is that why you hate the water?" she asks.

My legs feel heavy. Like they could pull the rest of me in the pool. And the rest of my body doesn't care.

I slide my foot back in.

"I mean, I do have a brother." It feels good to say it. I haven't told anyone here about Winston. "But he's dead."

Nia doesn't say anything. Nothing about being sorry, or any of those other awkward things people said to me at the funeral. She just looks at me. Patient. Like she knows there's more I want to say.

There is more. It's all been protected inside me. Waiting for someone to listen. Someone who won't say I'm crazy.

So I tell her.

I tell her why we'd never used our diving board or gone in the pool. I tell her how I never got to open my birthday presents that day. We spent the day at the hospital. And then we went home, without him. Mom started crying. She never really stopped.

Not until we moved here.

When I finish, she finally speaks. "Do you hate him?"

"No." Yes, sometimes. "I miss him."

"Of course you miss him." She shrugs. "But your whole life would have been different if he'd just done a cannonball."

"Or stayed out of the pool."

"Too boring." Nia swirls the water with pointed toes.

"You're right. Winston didn't know how to be boring."

I don't hate him for that. But she's right—sometimes I hate him for other things. For not being here. It feels like a broken promise. And sometimes I hate him for what happened after he died.

"My mom left us because of him." It comes out like a confession.

"Why? He was already gone."

"Not gone from her head. But my father was trying to make us forget."

I don't know how she found out. But one night, she confronted him. It was after we grilled burgers and ate corn on the cob. After she kissed me good night. After she closed the door to my room, so soft that you couldn't hear the latch click.

They yelled a lot that night. But nobody heard them except me. Our street was full of half-finished houses.

"You're erasing him!" she shouted. "You want us to forget he ever existed!"

Dad was just as loud. "You can't handle this on your own. All you talk about is Winston!"

I knew about the Messages before that night. I'd poked around in his study. Read things on his computer while he walked construction sites. It was strange. Interesting.

But I hadn't realized that the Messages were invented to fix us.

They said a lot of things that night. But there's one thing that I still think about, almost every day. Something Dad said. "Who's more important?" he asked. "The dead kid? Or the one who's still alive?"

I couldn't hear her answer. But she was gone in the morning.

Nia squeezes my hand, just for a second. "You can't forget loving somebody."

"The Messages can do anything." A shiver makes me wrap my arms around my middle.

"You're almost making me believe you," she says. "Except that it's impossible."

"It's true. Everyone has to listen to them. Me. You."

"Not me." She turns to look at me. Our noses nearly touch. "I only do what I want."

Only because she listens to the special Messages I made her. But I sense I shouldn't say it.

"Why are you here if you only do what you want?" I ask.

She lets out a long sigh and pulls back. Our faces are a polite distance now. "Part of me wanted to come."

"And the other part?"

"That part doesn't do what my parents want. Ever." She stares at me, eyes hard. "And they'd like nothing more than for me to hook up with you."

"You should do what it takes to make your parents happy," I say.

Wiggle my eyebrows to show it's a joke. But she's looking at the water now.

"My whole life, there's only been one thing I've wanted," she says. "Know what it is?"

Fantasies race through my mind. But I keep quiet and just shake my head.

"To do whatever my parents don't want." A little smile twists her lips. "And I'm very good at that."

"Like what?"

"It started with M&M's." She shoots me a sly look from the side of her eyes. "I used to buy a pound bag with my allowance and eat them on the way home from school. They were everything I wasn't supposed to have. Candy. Preservatives. And definitely not organic."

"Crazy girl."

"It got crazier." She swallows so hard I can hear it over the waterfall.

"You don't have to tell me."

"You told *me*." Nia shrugs. "Besides, you should know what a loser I am."

"You're not a—"

"Drinking. Drugs. Sex. Think of everything good Catholic parents don't want for their little girl. I did it all. Over and over again." She keeps her eyes on the water. "Now do you see what a loser I am? It wasn't even fun, most of it."

Because I don't. I'll never know what I would have been like, if I'd been given the chance to be normal. Everyone comes here screwed up some way. I would have been, too.

"I don't think you're a loser."

"I do." She says it quietly.

"But I think you should make up your own mind about what you want," I tell her.

She folds her arms over her stomach and kicks both feet up at the same time. "I only do what I want."

"No. You only do what pisses off your parents. Maybe you should do what you want—no matter if they'd like it or not."

Now she stares at me, hard. I return the look. "You're not scared of me."

"So quit trying," I tell her.

She edges closer. So do I. And then she kisses me.

It's soft. Slow. But it's like our bodies have been planning this. We press closer together. She rests one hand against my cheek, fingers spread out.

I can't hear anything except my breathing. And hers. The Messages are gone. But the rest of my brain is screaming. *Stop right now,* it warns me. *This is dangerous.*

Never get attached.

But she keeps going, and I keep going. I wonder how long we'll kiss. I wonder how long it will be before we do it again.

Dad could be coming home. He could walk out here and see this. But I don't stop.

She's the one who pulls away.

"We're not supposed to do that." Her voice is shaky.

"We don't have to tell."

She stands up and steps around me. Doesn't say anything else. She just goes to the steps at the shallow end of the pool. And walks in.

She doesn't stop to take off her shirt, or her pants, or even pull her hair back.

"Did I mention? I can't swim," she says.

"You need to get out." I'm on my feet. Looking for something, anything to pull her out. "Seriously. Get out."

She goes in deeper and deeper.

"I can't save you," I tell her.

She smiles and sweeps her hands across the surface. The water is over her waist.

"That's too deep. Come on. Get out."

"I can't swim." She throws me a grin. "But I can float."

Nia spreads her arms wide and falls back into the water. There's no splash. The water moves out of her way, then holds her.

She laughs. It bounces over the water and drowns out the sound of the waterfalls. "Come in, come in," she sings.

"I don't want to." A lie.

"The water is perfect." She looks ridiculous and beautiful. Her hair is fanned around her head. The white top clings to her body like wet tissue.

"My father could be home any second."

"You'll tell him I fell in."

Finally I find a pole with a net on the end. I stand on the top step and stretch it to her. "Take it. I'll pull you."

She grabs it. And tugs. Hard.

I stumble, down one step, then two. My breath flutters. I struggle to get it under control.

She tugs again. Another step down. Too far. Too deep.

But I don't let go.

"It's safe," she promises.

"You don't know how to swim," I remind her.

"But I bet you do. Even if you haven't done it for a long time."

She's right. I do know how to swim. Used to love it, even.

When she pulls again, I don't fight it. My body slides into the water without a splash. And then I'm next to her. Floating. Ridiculous and happy.

"Oops," she says. "You fell in, too."

I try to kiss her again. But she pushes me away.

"I know. Respectful space in every place," I mutter.

"Your girlfriend scares me."

"She won't hurt you."

"Unless she finds an ax in the bushes," she says.

Maybe she starts laughing first. Or maybe it's me. But then we're laughing together, the sound echoing off the rocks. It's louder than the pool pumps. The air conditioner. The mosquito truck that's circling the street.

That's when I decide. It only takes a second.

I want her here with me.

She doesn't have to leave. I can teach her how to pretend—let them think she's Candor perfect, like me. We'll know different.

We can hide in plain sight together.

"Maybe I should break up with Mandi," I say.

She rolls on her stomach and sticks her face in the water. Blows bubbles. When she pulls her head up, brown tendrils of hair are pasted to her face.

"Maybe you're right," she says. "But only if it's what *you* want."

I aim a splash of water at her. She pushes a wave right back.

I'll figure it out. How she'll stay. How she won't change. How I'll keep her safe. It all needs to be planned.

But not tonight.

Tonight, I'll just float.

chapter **12**

EVER SINCE NIA and I kissed, I've been trying to end things with Mandi. But she's always too busy to talk. After school, she's either studying or having a committee meeting for TAG. At night we can't talk. Her housekeeper answers the phone. "Miss Mandi has a test," she'll say. "She cannot be disturbed."

It's almost like Miss Mandi and I already broke up.

But it has to be official. And when I see the signs for the car wash, I make my move.

There's a car wash after school to benefit TAG. I'm not sure why she needs money for it. How much does a petition against graffiti cost? Can't her proud papa spring for a couple of clipboards and a package of printer paper?

Doesn't matter. I know I'll find her here. We'll talk. And then it will be over.

Some Candor clone boy is standing on Candor Ave., at the four-way stop by the SunStock Bank. He's holding a homemade sign. HELP TAG MAKE OUR CITY PRETTY. The letters are outlined in puff paint and colored in with pastel markers.

"You make that yourself?" I ask. It looks like something a Girl Scout would make to advertise cookies.

He juts his jaw out. "It's important to keep Candor beautiful."

Too bad the sign isn't helping his cause.

The tough face makes him look familiar. "Are you Tommy Kowalski?" I ask.

"Just Tom. You remember me, Oscar? You remember English class last semester, when we were partners on the vocab review?"

"Sure," I lie. "That was great."

What I do remember is when he moved here, almost a year ago. I'd never seen so many piercings. Studs lined his jaw. There were more in the web between his thumb and his finger. And he had a bar through the back of his neck. It made your skin itch to look, but you couldn't stop staring.

All the metal was gone six days after he moved here.

"Remember your nose ring?" I ask. "It was huge. You looked like a cow."

He shivers. "The past is best forgotten."

"Yeah. I thought you'd say that."

Tommy has a crew cut now, and he tucks his T-shirts into his shorts. All the way. I do, too, but only because it's my disguise. I wonder if part of Tommy knows he looks like a middle-aged guy with a minivan and three brats.

"Have you seen Mandi?" I ask him.

His eyebrows jerk up and down. There are knotty scars at the ends. "Why would you want to see her?"

Not the kind of hostile reaction I'm used to.

"Uh, because she's my girlfriend." For the next five minutes, at least.

"You don't belong together. You should stay away from her." He stares at me with narrow eyes.

If this weren't Candor, I would probably have to punch him out or something, for saying that. I'm not sure, since I've never been a teenager anywhere but here.

Besides, he's right.

"I'm going to break up with her," I tell him.

"Oh! Good idea!" He smiles, perfect even white teeth. Parents tend to fix their kids' outsides up, too, once Candor delivers their dream kid on the inside.

"Thanks, I guess."

He pulls out a walkie-talkie. I grab his hand. "Don't tell her it's me. She's avoiding me, I think."

"You promise you're breaking up?"

"Promise."

He grins and hits the button. "Corner Catcher to Mandi. Alpha customer headed your way."

"What's an alpha customer?"

"Big car with car seats. We charge extra for detailing. Mandi works out the deal." But then his face clouds. "Not that we rip people off. Never take advantage of someone else's need."

"I'm sure you're model citizens."

His radio crackles. "I'm at the hose hookups."

I follow the line of waiting cars for two blocks, until I'm at Pond-side Park. All the charity car washes are here. The town lets you use their water and their hoses.

Mandi's in the middle of everything. She points and kids scrub. I watch for a minute. Smooth blonde ponytail. Big pink-lipped smile. Shirt so loose, you can barely tell she's a girl. It's like she was made for Candor.

But it's the other way around. Candor made *her*.

Last year, during a long new-kid dry spell, I thought about changing that. Just a few Messages and she'd be hot for me. It could have been fun. She looks like the girl in a porno who shows up in a Velcro nurse costume. You know there's a bunch of bad under the white button-down shirt. Way under, in Mandi's case.

But I decided to skip it. I knew I could have fun with the new girls. My arrangement with Mandi was more important than sex. Being with her made me look good. And looking good kept me safe.

Maybe this is a stupid decision. Mandi kept me safe. But will Nia mean danger? Hasn't she already?

Truth is, I stopped being smart when she pulled me into the pool that night.

Tommy's right. Mandi should be with someone different. Someone who's pickled in the Messages, just like her.

Part of me will miss all the trying. Hold my hand, Mandi. Come kiss my cheek. Let me touch your hair. I always wondered if maybe she'd give in one day. It was an interesting experiment. Even if the results were always the same.

It'll be different with Nia. It already is.

Mandi spots me. "Oscar. We need to talk, but . . . I'm really busy."

"I'm the alpha customer," I tell her.

She looks up at the corner and I can tell Tommy's in trouble. I pull a twenty out of my pocket. "I told Tommy I wanted to donate to the cause."

Mandi's face relaxes. She sticks the money in her pocket. "We need more scrubbers. Come with me."

"Can't we just talk—?" But she's already ten feet ahead of me, like there's rocket fuel in the heels of her white sneakers. I rush to catch up.

Mandi leads me to a white car the size of a small elephant and hands me a hose. "I promised we'd get them all off."

The front of the beast is covered in smashed black bugs. "Not lovebugs," I groan. If you don't get them off right away, you're screwed.

"I know." Mandi shakes her head. "I should have charged extra."

Twice a year, the lovebugs appear. They float over the roads, and the grass, and the sidewalks. Always linked together. In bliss, until a semi smacks into them.

"At least they died happy," I say.

"They should have stayed in the bushes." Mandi looks over her shoulder. "What is Curtis doing? Doesn't he know—?" She sighs.

"Don't go yet. We have to talk. I'll be quick," I say. I hate that I'm begging. Especially her. But it's not for me, I remind myself. It's for Nia. It's for *us*.

"You're right. But I have to address this situation immediately." She bustles away. A skinny kid sees her coming and scrubs a hubcap double fast.

I aim my hose at the car. A few bug carcasses flake off. But mostly they stay on. A bead of sweat rolls under my Candor-crested polo. The sun is burning my scalp. If I'd known I was going to be outside, sweating like a gardener, I would have figured something else out. Like a letter. Or just telling Nia we broke up.

Never lie. The Message pops in, like I need to be reminded.

"You don't have to tell me," I mutter. Nia's worth more than that.

Mandi is back. She stands next to me with her hands on her hips. Inspects the car. "This still looks horrible. Or—um—perhaps you should work more on this."

"They're stuck. And I didn't come here to clean," I say.

"I have something difficult to say," she says. Glances over at the line of cars.

She can't fire me. I'd be her best worker, if I wanted to be. "Maybe if I had a different nozzle or a scrubby brush," I say. "I'm not saying I can't do it. It's just hard."

Mandi looks back at me. Her ponytail sways a little with the motion. "Sometimes . . ." She sighs and presses her lips together, staring at me. "Sometimes, Oscar, people's paths diverge. It's nobody's fault when a romance dissolves."

Is she talking about us? I know we don't belong together. But since when does *she* think that?

Maybe she really *was* avoiding me.

"Who's—um—dissolving?" I ask.

"Am I being kind? It's important to end relationships gently." She stares, waiting for me to reply.

Messages, ones I don't remember hearing before, drop reminders in my brain. First there's what Mandi just said: *End relationships gently.* Then *Recognize when it's time to move on.* I've been programmed for this occasion and I didn't even realize it.

"You're doing fine," I tell her. It's like she has a script.

"It's time for us to go our separate ways." She squints at me. "Don't you think?"

This isn't how it was supposed to go. I was going to break the news. She was going to be sad. Or at least annoyed. Maybe even a little rude. "Aren't you upset?" I ask.

"It's not like we were in love." Then she claps her hand over her mouth. "Oh, Oscar. Were you—are you—?"

"No. I wasn't. I'm not." I never loved her. Just appreciated the cover.

"I'm not doing this right. I woke up early this morning and practiced for hours."

It's been eating me, too. But I thought it was guilt. "How about we just say we broke up."

"Oh. Oh! Yes. That's a good idea, if it's acceptable to you." She swings the clipboard to one hip and holds out the other hand. "Thank you, Oscar. You were a good boyfriend."

I drop the hose and wipe my hand. And then I shake her hand. What else am I supposed to do? I don't know. She was my first girl-friend. And now she's my first breakup.

"So we can see other people?" I ask.

"Of course we can." Mandi looks back at the workers. I can tell she's thinking. Plotting. "I like having a boyfriend."

"Just not me."

She tilts her head. "Are you sure you're okay?"

"It's fine. I was going to break up with you anyway," I say.

"Of course." She shrugs. "Mandi and Oscar don't belong to-gether."

"Everyone knows that," I say. I'm starting to wonder how— why—everyone knows that.

She takes a step back and looks at the bug specks. "Before you go, get the rest off. Those things are disgusting."

I realize I'm still holding the hose. Water is dribbling from the end, making a puddle around my feet.

Mandi takes a few steps away. But then she turns to look at me. "I mean, please can you do that?"

I can't help laughing. Watching the Messages jerk her around has been interesting. "Since you said 'please.'"

"You weren't so bad." Her smile relaxes into something more real, until it's almost gone. "I hope you'll be happy."

Then I'm left hosing dead lovebugs off a car, for my ex-girlfriend, in soppy Florida heat. Am I being nice because I feel guilty? Or sad?

Or is it because the Messages are making me?

It's been a river that's been running through my brain for days.

Mandi and I don't belong together. I have to break up with Mandi. I thought it was because of Nia. Because I was sick of pretending.

But now I wonder. Did my father decide this for me?

I blast the rest of the black bodies off the grille. Even hose off the hubcaps, too. It's satisfying. I'm doing this because I want to, I decide.

And from now on, I'll be sure. Everything I'm doing will be what I want.

Starting with Nia.

chapter 13

DATING IS DIFFERENT in Candor.

At least I think it is. I never had a date anywhere else. But I know it has to be . . . sexier, in the real world. Or at least more fun. Otherwise nobody would reproduce.

Most kids go to the movies. I guess that's like other places. But here, we share a cardboard boat of carrot sticks. Popcorn could kill you: greasy, salty, and let's not think about the choking risk.

A

Everyone gets their own cartons of milk. It's not sanitary to share drinks. We all know that.

The movies are always G-rated. The armrests don't slide up, and they're half a foot wide. Plenty of room to balance your carrot sticks. And an SAT review book with a flashlight, if you're Mandi.

You can take your date other places, too. There's the ice-cream parlor, which should be called the fat-free-sugar-free-yogurt parlor. Everyone sits and acts like everyone else.

Or you can go for a walk. One foot apart at all times, of course. Respectful space in every place.

I don't want those kinds of dates with Nia.

I want our first date to be special. Something to make her see that I'm different. That she's different. We don't have to be like everyone else in Candor.

At first I thought we'd go to a museum. An art museum, with old paintings and things made by dead people. She'd love it.

There's a big museum in Sarasota, where Mom took me before the Messages told her not to. I'll drive us there. We'd eat french fries and chocolate shakes and I'd kiss Nia again.

We would be back by night. Before Dad noticed.

But the Messages stopped me.

Everything you need is in Candor.

Stay close to Candor.

They flooded my brain, covering Sarasota and chocolate shakes. The only people who don't get treated to those Messages are the kids headed for college. There's probably a whole special Message pack to keep them in line.

The rest of us tend not to leave much. No vacations. No stolen afternoons at an art museum.

If it's this hard for me, it would be worse for Nia. She definitely wouldn't want to go.

So I made plans for a secret date, right here in Candor.

She's coming to the shed late. Sneaking out. Taking risks, like me. It's worth it.

I zigzag twine across the ceiling of the shed. Then I reach for the stack of papers and a clothespin.

My first selection is a painting of a girl holding a string. A bird is attached to the other end. It's trying to fly away. But the girl just laughs.

The girl's not nice. But I like her anyway. Maybe it's her pink lips, or her full cheeks. She's beautiful, like Nia.

I pull another sheet from the pile and clip it to the twine. The ripped edges of the paper feel soft, like feathers.

The box was in the garage. It was moldy. Nobody had touched it since Mom left.

ART BOOKS. It was written on top in pink marker. Mom's handwriting.

I picked the one from the museum in Sarasota. It was full of glossy pictures—paintings, sculptures, ancient copper necklaces. I ripped every single picture out.

I pin up another picture. Another. The zigzags fill with paper. It hangs straight down. Every time I move to hang one up, they flutter. It's the only sound in the shed.

But there will be music. My music, with the special Messages. I pull open the pegboard and slide the CD into my player. It's classical music. Pianos and violins.

There are a few new Messages. Things about staying. Never telling on someone you love. It's insurance. I won't get caught and neither of us will be lonely.

There's a knock. A pause. Three fast knocks.

It's Nia.

I open the door a crack and push my hand through. "Close your eyes," I whisper. Her hand is soft. I feel the delicate bones under her skin when I tug her inside.

Her hair is in braids twisted on her head. She's wearing little sparkly earrings and jeans that look glued to her hips. I step close and smell lilacs, warm, like summer.

"Open." I'm still whispering, even though the door is closed and locked.

Her eyes get big, bigger. She steps forward and touches one of the pages dangling from the twine. "It's a museum," she says.

I can't help grinning. "Exactly."

I watch as she slides away from me. She looks. No, more than that. Drinks. Her eyes drink in the art like she's been in a desert.

She ducks under a row of paper and steps to the next one. "Rubens!" she says. "And Cairo! Cairo's *Judith*! How did you know?"

She's holding a picture of a girl who's wearing a turban. The girl has a sword stuck through a man's head.

"I guess it's nice," I say. If you like homicidal maniacs.

"She's so pale." Nia sighs and her hand drops. "It's a perfect contrast. Look at the shadows."

"You're better," I say. "You could paint that."

I mean it. But again she laughs. "Go find your favorite," she says. "Stop telling me such lies."

"This is for you. Not me."

"I thought you said it was a date?" Her smile makes my mouth dry.

"It's our first date."

"Then leave me alone and look for yourself. You don't just follow someone around a museum, not even on a date." She gives me a smile and a small shove. "Even if you are cute."

I stagger back and slap my hand over my chest. "You wound me."

She just laughs and waves me away. "Be gone, Picasso."

Tuesday afternoons used to be museum day, in Chicago. Winston had Boy Scouts. So Mom and I picked a different museum every week. It was just her and me.

She made looking at art into a game. "Find a dog," she'd say. "Find a picture of a train."

I ran from room to room. When I found something, I grabbed her hand and dragged her there. She laughed, even when the guards stared at us. We weren't supposed to make noise. But we didn't care.

"Did you find something good?" Nia asks.

"Not yet." I start down another zigzag row. There's a lion, staring. A lot of fat angels with wings.

One makes me want to look more. It's a bridge arched high over water. There's a tiny man walking across, leading a donkey. The full moon lights his way. "I wonder where they're going," I say.

Nia comes over to look. "He's running away."

"Or going home."

"It's whatever you want it to be," she says. "That's why I like art. Nobody's wrong."

He's stuck there forever. Three inches away from somewhere else. The picture looks darker now. Like the moon is going under a cloud.

"There's a better one," I tell her.

She follows me to the middle of the room, where all the pieces of twine cross. Like a nest.

"It's different from the others," I say. A pencil drawing, hanging from the very center. Not glossy. Not ripped from a book.

She brushes it with one fingertip. Her eyes flit to the other ones. "My drawing?"

"It belongs here."

She gives her head a tiny shake. "I wish you could see my oil portraits. Or the watercolors I did last year."

"The museum would be proud to display more of your work," I say. "We accept donations at all times."

"It's all gone." Nia wraps her arms around herself.

I slide one arm around her shoulders. She doesn't step away and I feel a warm flush. A girl who wants me to touch her, all on her own. "What happened?"

She sighs. "It all looked so ugly. All I could think was, *Art is useless*. It went through my head over and over."

One of my father's Messages. My teeth are clenched so tight, my temples hurt.

"So I threw them out. It filled up the entire trash can." A sad half smile is on her face. "My parents helped. It made them happy, and I still did it."

"When?"

"Last week." She pulls in a shuddering breath and looks around. "I wish I'd kept them."

"It's okay," I tell her. Even though it's not. Even though I want to hurt my father for hurting her. For taking away what she loved the most. "You'll make new ones."

Even with my Messages, she's changing. I need more time— time for her to listen to my music, not his. I'll play music whenever we're together. I'll give her new CDs, ones with stronger Messages.

"Let's talk about something else." She taps another painting.

It's a couple. His face is turned away to face his girl. I can tell he's staring. Like he can't ever see enough. Her arm is draped around his shoulder and she's saying something. Pointing. Like she's explaining something.

"It's us," she says.

"You're prettier."

She snorts. "I'm not even as pretty as the flower on her hat."

"Do you like it?" I ask.

I mean the room. The music. Being with me. But she tugs the paper free. "I love it."

Then she folds it into halves, quarters, halves again. Sticks it in her pocket.

"You're an art thief," I say.

"Well, there's no gift shop. Besides, I know the guard." She steps close.

The rest is so easy. We kiss. She slides her hand through my hair. I wrap my arm around her waist. It feels too small.

I've kissed other girls in the shed—new ones that I knew would be leaving soon. But not like this. Not like it mattered.

Her lips are soft. I slide a thumb over her cheek. Her skin is even softer. I want to touch it more. And more. But I feel like I'll ruin it, ruin her, somehow. I only want to do things that make her better.

The Messages trickle in. Weak at first. Then hard to ignore. Pounding against my defenses. Looking for the breaking point. The same ones that are always warning me.

Respectful space in every place.

Avoid physical contact.

I push them away. *You don't own me,* I tell them. *I do what I want.*

But then Nia yanks her head back. She wipes her mouth with her fingers and makes a face, like I taste bad. "Only husbands and wives kiss," she gasps.

It feels like she punched me. I know it's not fair. She doesn't know her thoughts don't belong to her. And she lasted a long time.

I want to explain. Remind her about the Messages. But what if she believes me this time? Nia's impossible to predict. But I'm sure she'd be furious. She hates anything or anyone who tries to control her.

What I don't know is whether she'd tell. Who she'd talk to. What damage she'd leave behind.

My father would feel compelled to fix things.

Then I'd lose her before I even had a chance with her.

Besides, there's a new Message playing. One to make her forget the truth about the Messages. To keep us both safe.

So I point at the bowl of M&M's by the chairs. "The museum has a snack bar."

It's my special stash, from two clients ago. I've been saving it for a special occasion.

"You remembered?" Nia holds one up and inspects it. "Are these real?"

I take a handful and pop them in my mouth. "They're real."

"Only eat nutritious food." But she doesn't put it down.

"Just eat one. Because you want to."

She slides the single M&M onto her tongue. Her lips close. Then her eyes. She lets out a big sigh.

"Better than nutritious," I say.

"Keep it this way," she says. "Forever. I want to come here every night and look at art and eat chocolate."

And be together, I want her to say. But she just eats another M&M.

Tonight we can pretend. "I'll name it the Nia Museum and charge admission," I tell her.

Her hand hovers over the bowl. She picks a green one. "That's three. I'll save it for later."

"Eat it and take more."

"I shouldn't. I can't." She looks at her watch. "It's so late."

"Just one more minute."

She stays. I sit on the chair. Nia sits on my lap. Not crazy, like a lap dancer. Just light, sideways, like she could hop away any second.

The Messages pound in my head. But I kiss her anyway.

Nia pulls away, then presses close again.

One minute becomes five. Fifteen.

The sprinklers switch on outside. Nia jumps off.

I stand up. "You have to go."

She looks around the room. Then she shuts her eyes. Her eyes are full of tears when she looks at me again. "I memorized it," she says. "So I can remember forever."

"We can remember tomorrow," I tell her. "Together."

But the door is already closed behind her.

chapter 14

TODAY'S BRICK DAY. The new families get their engraved brick near the flagpole. They clap. They cry. They feel like they finally belong.

It's different for me. Brick Day is a reminder of how Dad and I are different. That we're missing half of what made us a family.

"Tarp's almost too small." Dad nudges the green plastic tarp over the bricks with his freshly polished loafer. "We'll need a new one next year. Be sure to tell Calvin."

"I already did," I tell him. It won't be cheap: a custom-made tarp with the Candor seal in the middle, cut through on one side so two people—always Dad and me—can pull it away. But cost doesn't matter to Dad when it comes to public shows.

"Good man. We're the same, aren't we?" Dad swings one arm over my shoulder and pulls me close, just for a second.

He's being nicer than usual, with nobody watching. I wonder if he feels what I'm feeling. The urge to remember her today.

I want this over as soon as possible.

You get a brick when you move to Candor. It's engraved with whatever you want. Most people put the names of their family and the year they moved here. A few get cute with a little saying or a pun.

But you don't keep the brick. Dad's people store them in the Milton model's garage. Then, once a year, they pull up some of the blank bricks in the patio around the town flagpole. The engraved ones are installed. The people who have lived here the longest are closest to the pole. The newest ones are at the edge. It's like tree rings.

"They look good," Dad says. "People should be pleased."

"Always strive to satisfy the customer," I parrot back. It doesn't have to be a Message. I've heard him say it so many times it has its own spot engraved in my brain.

The ceremony is the same every year. Dad will make a speech. Then we'll pull the tarp off. Slow and dramatic.

People will clap.

Someone always cries.

Helping him has always been my job. Maybe it would have been Mom's. But she was gone a long time before the first Brick Day.

Even though she kind of invented it.

I push the thought away. Not this year. I won't even look. I'll be wrecked for the day. The week, even. Drinking sparkling apple cider in the dark shed and listening to her favorite music—old coffeehouse crap—until two in the morning.

Not this year. I will not give in to any of it this time.

It's not even eleven, but thick clouds are climbing over our heads. Lucky for me. "Maybe we should start early," I tell Dad. "A storm's coming."

"We'll wait until everyone is here," he says.

Wouldn't want a single person to miss Dad's golden words.

The first family drives up in their shiny new NEV. Every family drives Neighborhood Electric Vehicles here. Better for the environment. And they're gosh-darn cute, like golf carts but curvier, painted any way the owner wants.

The adults go up to Dad. Their kid comes up to me. He's ten, maybe, with a fresh haircut. "You're Oscar Banks."

I give him a wave. Try to smile nice. "Superior citizen at your service."

"Someday I'm going to be just like you." He studies me like he's memorizing something.

"It's too hard. Maybe try being an astronaut. Or a racecar driver," I tell him. Haircut shakes his head. Giggles. Runs back to his parents.

More people come. Dad does adult duty and I handle the kids. A couple come close to kissing my hand, I swear. I tell them all about the exciting spread at the community center afterward: carrot juice and bran bars.

There's a miraculous break. Nobody's talking to me. Then Nia's in front of me.

Her hair is brushed into a smooth ponytail, like the other girls. But her jeans are so tight, I don't know how she sits. And she's wearing these tall rainbow flip-flop things that look like a definite safety hazard when running.

She only half passes. It's too dangerous. I need to help her blend. But how do I do that without explaining everything?

"I don't get the bricks," she says.

"Everybody loves something with their name on it." I tell her. "You'll cry when you see yours."

"Only if it gets dropped on my foot."

"They're already in here. Stuck forever." I point at the tarp. "Want to peek?"

"I can stand the suspense." She rolls her eyes. It makes me look around, worried. What if Dad notices her attitude? He might take bigger steps to fix her. Or blame me. Either would be bad.

"How long will this take?" she asks.

"Not long. It's not awful." I feel like I need to defend it, suddenly. Loyal Brick Boy. Why?

Nia leans close to whisper. "I was in the middle of drawing something. I don't want my fingers to forget where they were going." Then she traces one long finger over the back of my hand.

It feels good. Too good. Too public. I pull my hand back fast, like she's a hot stove. "People might see," I say.

"If that's how you want it, Picasso." Her eyes look mad—squinty and small.

"I want to be with you. Just . . . not here. Somewhere private."

She looks down at her feet, then back up. "The woods, then," she says. "Ten o'clock."

Dangerous. There's no music in the woods. And there are animals. Big ones. I wasn't lying to Sherman about the boars.

"How about the golf course?" I ask.

"The woods. Or nowhere."

I don't want to sit at home tonight. Think about what I missed. I nod. "Ten o'clock. Meet you at the boardwalk behind the school."

"I can't wait." Nia looks back at her parents. "We could go now."

"I have to be here," I tell her.

"Have it your way." Nia purses her lips. "I'll just go hang with my generous sponsors." And then she struts over to her parents. I regret it right away, although the back view is a don't-miss.

I feel someone staring. I look around.

Sherman is here. He's standing just behind a woman who must be his mother, close enough that their bodies must be touching. There's a movement near her hip. I realize Sherman is holding his mother's hand.

Then she looks at him and cups her other hand on his cheek. I can't hear what she says, but she smiles. All proud, like he's such a prize.

What kind of freak teenage boy holds his mother's hand, especially in public? What kind of mother encourages that? Even brainwashed, he's an impossible dork.

I know I should go over there and make nice, like a truly superior citizen would. But I think I'd vomit all over his green Candor polo. So I just look away before they start making out.

It's getting windier. The tarp ripples as the wind moves across it, makes loud snapping noises. Dad's staring up at the sky. Then he looks at me. Like he's asking a question.

It makes me feel proud for a second. Like we're partners. I give him a nod.

Let's get this going, it says.

Dad raises up his arms. "Folks," he says. "We're getting started!"

The crowd gets quiet. We gather in a circle around the tarp. Then we all hold hands without being told to. That happens every year. And Messages have nothing to do with it. People are just feeling all gooey-gushy.

Dad's on one side of me. A woman with sweaty hands is on the other side. Her hand moves inside mine every time she shifts.

He makes some jokes about the clouds coming to see the bricks, too. People laugh like he's a Vegas headliner. Then it's the standard speech.

But I'm not listening, really. Nia is standing right across from me. She's holding hands, too. Her mother is on one side, nodding to everything Dad says. Her father is on the other side. He's tall like Nia, with her curly hair.

She won't look at me. So I get lost staring at her lips. Blood-red today. Never smiling. Another way she's out of sync.

What will we do in the woods tonight? How many rules can we break?

I almost miss my cue to remove the tarp. But Dad drops my hand, and that tells me. It's time for Brick Boy to do his job.

We walk away from each other, around the circle. People ripple back to let us pass with the tarp. Then they move forward again.

All the bricks are revealed. At first the crowd stands on the edge, not stepping on the bricks. Craning their necks to find theirs.

But soon they aren't shy. They walk on the bricks and dodge around each other. Desperate, I think, to find theirs.

Proof that they belong.

Soon flashes from tiny digital cameras are going off. A couple of proud-Dad types in jean shorts point their video cameras toward the brick. One even has a fancy TV-style light that illuminates everything in front of him like a floodlight. "The family brick," he says in a deep voice. "Installed today, here forever."

Dad is helping people find their bricks. He never has to ask what their name is. I know I should do it, too; at least, I always have.

But I feel that one brick pulling me in. So I step away, away, until I'm off the patio and on the grass.

Nia. I'll watch her. She'll keep me in the present.

That doesn't last long. She says something to her parents. Her mother's face tightens, but then she shakes her head. Like she's saying, Fine, do what you want.

Nia turns and walks away from the crowd. Three steps over perfect green grass. Then she stops and looks over her shoulder.

Our eyes meet. She beckons with one finger.

Come. Come right now. Away from this, with me.

The invitation I wanted, the day she drew me at the park. I look at my father. Wonder what would happen if I followed her.

By the time I look back, she's walking away. It seems too late to go with her.

There's a loud boom. All the Florida newbies jump. One woman screams, like we don't get thunderstorms every day.

"Don't forget the reception at the community center," Dad calls out. "There are lots of tasty, healthy treats!"

They hurry to their NEVs. The new people don't live close enough to the town center to walk to the bricks. All the new houses get built along the edges. Like the bricks.

All we have to do is walk two blocks home.

But Dad steps closer to the flagpole.

"It's not safe," I say. "There's lightning."

"Just for a minute," he says.

If he's looking, I have to. I walk over. We face each other, the brick between us.

Campbell, Lucy, and Oscar: proud first citizens of Candor

Her name, trapped with us forever. It's the closest thing we have to a tombstone for her. I wonder if it's why he didn't try to make me forget like with Winston: there's proof.

It makes me feel ten years old again. Remembering one of the last happy days.

But I don't like to remember. It reminds me of how different things are now.

Ours was the first brick, of course. Mom made us come here together. She brought a bottle of sparkling apple cider. It was so hot outside.

She opened the bottle and dripped some of the liquid on the bricks. It fizzed and boiled away. "We are officially official," she said. Her voice was lighter than it had been for a long time. Almost like the weight of Winston being dead was gone.

"Great. Now it'll get ants," Dad said.

But Mom laughed—she never took him seriously. At least, not until she was mad enough to leave. "Ceremony is important. Isn't it, Oscar?"

Her wink made me feel like I was enough. Me and apple cider on a brick.

I nodded.

And Dad smiled. "Maybe you're right. We should do a ceremony for everyone."

"What an outstanding idea," she said. "We'll get everyone drunk on apple cider and expensive real estate."

But of course she never made it to a single ceremony. It was just strangers clumped around Dad and me. They were like ants drinking our fake sweetness. Not knowing the difference.

When we walked home that last happy day, Mom was in the middle. I held one arm, like I was escorting her to a ball. Dad held the other.

She showed us how to be happy.

And we forgot after she left.

"It hasn't changed at all," Dad says. "It looks like it was installed yesterday."

The image of Nia leaving flashes in my mind. The beckoning finger. An invitation to be different.

It makes me brave enough to say what I've always wanted to.

"Why didn't you ever change the brick?"

Dad keeps his eyes on the ground. "We never change the bricks."

"But—you're you. And she's gone. You could change it."

Dad passes one hand over his face, wiping the rain away. It's getting heavier now. Soon the skies will open. "Your mother was here at the start."

Then he looks at me. "Do you miss her? Do you—?" A bitter smile twists his lips. "Do you need her?"

He has never asked me that question. Not once.

"Not anymore, I guess. . . ." I swallow and give him the truth, for once. "I guess sometimes I still *want* her, though."

Dad crosses his arms and nods once. He's looking across the patio at the park now. Like he can see far away. "I'm sorry I couldn't get her to stay."

"You could have if you wanted to."

Another boom of thunder. Lightning streaks behind him, turning the sky pink for a split second.

None of it is as scary as the sharp look he gives me. Like he sees what's inside my head. He knows that I know. I'm sure of it, in that second.

"I mean, if you'd asked her to stay—" The words rush out of my mouth. Trying to fix what I said. Things need to be normal, safe, again.

He clears his throat. "I did everything I could."

"I know. I'm sure. I'm sorry." I sound desperate. It's not an act.

More thunder. It seems to change him back to the man I know now. Dad straightens his body and squares his shoulders, like he's putting on a new suit. "You are a young man with great advantages," he says. His voice is heavy. A warning. "You should be grateful."

"I am. I am always grateful for my circumstances." I feed the Message to him fast.

"All this family needs is Candor." Dad looks down at the brick one more time. "Nobody and nothing is missing."

He turns and walks off the patio. But I stay for a minute. Watch all the names fill with water. I imagine it freezing. The bricks would break. All the history inside would be gone.

But nothing freezes in Florida except busted air conditioners. These bricks are here forever. And I have to deal with it—or forget they exist.

When I look up, Dad beckons with his finger. Just like Nia did.

But this time is different.

This time I obey.

chapter **15**

WE MEET IN a dark corner of the boardwalk.

"I know a safe place in the woods," I tell her. There are old platforms in the trees, where hunters used to sit. No boars. No prying eyes.

"Forget it," she says. "We're going to *my* place tonight."

Relief. Her house is safe. But I did think tonight would be fun. The kind of fun I'm not supposed to have.

She starts jogging down the boardwalk. Away from her house.

"Wrong way," I shout.

Nia doesn't slow. Just looks behind to make sure I follow.

Which I do. Even if I have no idea where we're going. Which is obviously *not* her place, unless we're taking a five-mile detour through the swamp.

It's a typical night: warm and humid. But the normal Candor sounds fade as we get deeper into the woods. No more air conditioners or hissing sprinklers. The shrill frogs get louder. Our footsteps echo on the hollow wooden floor of the boardwalk.

My heavy backpack moves up and down with every step. It's got a boom box inside, with music. And a tasty beverage from my stash.

I run smack into the middle of a cobweb. "Can we slow down?" I call out, wiping the nastiness from my face.

"Almost there!" she answers.

About five minutes later, she stops. Looks up and around. Then nods.

"This is the place." She swings over the waist-high fence that's on either side of the boardwalk. Looks at me. Waiting for me to leap into the preserve, with the snakes and the boars and—

And the hot girl.

I jump. She slides her hands over my eyes.

"It's a surprise," she whispers.

We stumble through the undergrowth. I trip, once. But she grabs my shoulders to steady me. I open my eyes and look around, but it's just woods. At least it's a full moon. I can see the palm trees and vines.

"Close them." She puts her hands back. Her palms are cool against my cheeks.

When she finally drops her hands, we're still in the woods. But there's something here, in the middle of the croaking frogs and spiderwebs. Something that doesn't belong.

"Did you build this?" I ask.

"Yes." Nia looks at me, a big smile on her face. "I wanted to have a special place, somewhere besides the shed. Something that belongs to us."

She says "us" like it's got a capital letter in it.

Nia built us a house. Well, more like a lean-to. It's made of dead branches and topped with palm fronds. The tallest part of the roof is about four feet high, and it slopes to the ground from there. A lantern hangs under the roof. Inside, on the ground, there's a red blanket topped with a picnic basket.

Someone could have found it.

She could have been caught.

But I know those aren't the things I'm supposed to say. Besides, nobody comes out here except the boars and the snakes.

"We need music." For our addicted brains—and hopefully to keep the wildlife away. I set down the boom box and hit the play button. Soft guitars. It doesn't fit with the frogs, but it's all I brought. And we can't stay out here without it.

"That's all? *We need music?* I got blisters building this thing." Nia grabs my hand. "Come on, I'll give you the grand tour."

She lights the lantern. Shows me how she tied the branches together with rope.

"I even scratched our initials in it." Nia takes my finger and rubs it over the highest part of the roof. I can feel the marks, even if I can't read them.

If it was daylight, anyone could see them. Maybe guess at what they mean.

People know we're together. But nobody knows why she's been so slow to change. Or that I'm using Messages to keep her that way.

Not even Nia knows that part. Guilt closes my throat. I've almost told her a hundred times. But I'm afraid of what she'll say.

She might not understand.

"Do you like it?" she asks. Her voice sounds like she really cares. Like I could hurt her with my answer.

I feel the scratched initials again. She made this for me. For us. If she didn't love me, this place wouldn't exist. It would still be a pile of dead sticks.

"It's beautiful. And solid," I tell her. "This thing could last forever."

"Come inside. I want to show you something else." She makes me sit on the blanket first, then sits across from me. It's so tight under the roof that our knees touch.

Then she opens the picnic basket.

Pulls out a plastic tub full of cookies—homemade, it looks like. And then some brown teacups and a glass container full of liquid. "Iced tea," she says.

"We're having a tea party?" I ask. Surprised.

She giggles. It sounds different from her usual laugh. Lighter. Younger.

But nice.

"I thought you had some big bad plans," I tell her.

The smile drops off her face. I'm a jerk. It wasn't supposed to come out like that.

But I was looking forward to at least one of my fantasies coming true. Any of them. I'm not picky.

A tea party in the woods wasn't on my list.

"This is special." Nia fingers one of the cups.

"You're right. I just—I never pictured you being a tea party kind of girl."

"I used to have tea parties with my boyfriends all the time."

That doesn't fit the Nia Silva dossier in Dad's files. I'm so confused, I just stare.

"Bubba Bear and Lolly the Giraffe were more polite than you. You eat more, too," she says.

Then she leans over the basket. Our lips meet. I do my best to prove I beat Bubba Bear in the tea-party-date department. In all departments.

We take our time.

Forget my fantasies. This is good. This is very good.

She pulls away too soon. It's always too soon. But I'll take what I can get, anything I can get, from her.

"Your cup." She hands me a brown cup with a stick attached to the side, like a handle. I hold it close to the lantern to get a better look.

"Is this bark?" I ask.

"Birch bark," she answers.

"You made a lean-to and cups, too?"

"Not exactly. I made these when I was eight." Nia examines her cup with a small smile. "I called them my fairy cups."

"Do they work?"

She answers by pouring some tea in mine. "I made it sweet, like when I was little."

I take a sip. The sugar from the tea coats my lips. But nothing leaks out of the cup.

Nia fills her cup, too. We're quiet. I stare at her while I force the tea down. Her hair looks almost red under the lantern. And soft.

"I found the cups while I was unpacking. They gave me this whole idea," she says.

"It was a good idea." I take another tiny sip of tea. It's nice out here. I could almost believe Candor didn't exist—if it weren't for my guitar music playing.

"The cookies taste better than the tea," she says.

"No, the tea's great," I lie.

Little lies are fine—aren't they? Ones that make her feel good?

But what about the big lies? The ones that protect her? Aren't those okay, too?

She gulps the rest of her tea and takes my cup. "I'll finish yours. Have a cookie."

The cookie is bad in a very good way—like her. Packed with chocolate chips. Walnuts. So much butter my father would have a panic attack. Watch out, arteries.

"You made these?" I ask.

"All by myself." She flutters her eyelashes.

Nia's domestic. I never knew that.

And I love it. Maybe that makes me a typical pig guy. But who wouldn't love a girl who feeds him chocolate—especially when his typical dessert is half a banana?

"Have more," she says.

I take two.

"Don't get used to this girlfriend-baking-you-cookies thing," she says. "I quit baking a long time ago."

Which is kind of a relief. My Nia is still inside the baking goddess.

"I can make you rye toast," I tell her.

"Pass." She grabs another cookie.

"What else did you do when you were eight?" I ask.

"All good things. Being eight was the best," she says.

I nod. "When I was eight, I had a brother. And a mother." Everything would change in two years. But I didn't know it then.

What changes are coming now? What don't I know about?

Nothing can be as bad as losing Mom and Winston.

"When I was eight, I hadn't screwed anything up yet," Nia says slowly.

"I was a Boy Scout. Big shock, huh?"

She answers me with a long kiss. I run my hands down her bare arms. Shoulders to elbows to wrists. She has goose bumps, even in the muggy Florida night.

Maybe that's because of me.

Sometimes I forget she likes me the same way I like her.

When we stop, Nia is smiling. "I was in Girl Scouts."

"Sure you were. Was it a special troop with black uniforms?"

She gives me a little shove. "No! And I earned a ton of badges."

"For what?" I picture what she'd get them for now. Cutting class. Kissing with tongue. Making beautiful art.

"I got them for all kinds of things—camping, running a lemonade stand, helping old people." Nia runs her finger across and down her front, like she's touching a sash. "My favorite was the pet-care one, because it had a cat on it."

"Did you have a pet?"

"Just the fish Mom bought me, so I could do the badge. It died. But they let me have the badge anyway."

"Killing a fish sounds like a pretty major screwup," I tease.

She's staring off into space. Answers slowly. "No. I was a really good Girl Scout."

"I can't picture it." All I can imagine is a miniature Nia. Long wild hair and ripped jeans, with baby army boots. And, I guess, a green sash.

"Then I started to change." Nia lifts the container of tea. "More?"

Bravely, I nod.

She laughs. Dumps the rest outside of the lean-to.

"Why'd you stop being good?" I ask.

She's told me what she's done. But she never explains why it happened.

"Being good got less interesting." She shrugs.

"I know what you mean." I eye her tank top.

"But now . . ." Her voice trails off. I meet her eyes.

She looks down at the ground. Shy, suddenly.

"What?" I ask.

When she doesn't answer, I take her hand. Gentle. But firm enough to let her know I'm there. Listening.

"You make me feel like I'm eight," she says. "Like I want to be good again."

What do I say? Do I tell her it's not me? It's the Messages? Would she love me less?

Maybe even hate my guts?

"If someone like you loves me . . ." Her tongue stumbles a little over the L-word.

"Which I do."

"Then I might be worth something. Even after all the stupid things I've done." She lets out a shaky laugh. Uses her other hand to brush tears from her eyes.

How can she not see how amazing she is?

"You're worth something. You're worth everything," I tell her. "I'd do anything for you."

"Me, too."

I'm holding both her hands now. Like we're making vows to each other.

Now is the time to tell her everything.

Convince her the Messages are real—even though my own Messages have been telling her differently.

Confess to feeding her my own words. Helping her to fight. But not giving her a chance to do it herself.

We lean closer. Closer. Her lips move down my neck. Her tongue flicks, teases.

I could push her away. Tell her we have to talk.

"I love you," I say weakly.

"I love you, too," she whispers.

Now her mouth is hovering over mine. If I don't say something now, the moment will be gone. We'll be too busy doing other things.

Things I'm not going to stop until she does.

She closes the gap. I don't stop her. I don't say anything.

Instead I pull her closer, and we fall on the blanket, on top of the wood cups. There's a small cracking sound.

"They broke," Nia says.

"We'll make more," I tell her.

"It doesn't matter."

We go back to kissing. And touching. We stay in the woods a long time.

It's a perfect night. Or it would be, if I didn't feel guilty.

But if that's the price to pay for keeping her, I'll live with it.

chapter 16

HER TOES ARE on my ankle. Traveling up my leg. Under my pants. Soft, tickling toes. Naked naughty toes.

"Stop that." I say it over the noise of the Messages warning me. They're louder when we're not in the woods. "I mean—please stop that."

Nia drops her foot like she's wearing a lead boot. "I thought you were my boyfriend."

"Not here. Don't do that here."

We're in the rocking chairs at Pondside Park, studying. Which means Nia's distracting me, and I'm trying to keep her from blowing my cover.

Sort of. The distractions aren't so bad.

But there are people everywhere. They all know the rules. I don't want them seeing me—me, Campbell Banks's kid—breaking them.

"You weren't so boring last night." Nia tucks both feet under her. The pianos from my custom Message mix get louder, for a second. I have the player in my backpack feeding us the good stuff.

"We were safe then," I tell her. "But we should have studied in the dining room today."

She doesn't meet my eyes. Her pencil is roaming over her sketchbook, leaving curved gray trails behind it.

"Things are different in public," I say. "We're not safe."

Nia snorts and flips to a fresh page. "Are you still trying to sell me on those secret . . . M . . . M . . ." Her mouth looks like it's glued shut.

The boosters I keep giving her are working. They undo my big mistakes. I never should have told her the truth. What if she'd believed me? What if she'd told?

Worse—what if Dad had gotten ahold of her and "fixed" things?

We're meant to be together.

An older man with a Red Sox cap sits in the chair closest to Nia. He nods his head at me and I roll out my flawless good-kid smile.

"Don't you have math homework? I could help." I say it loud enough for the man to hear.

"Screw math." Nia looks at me, finally. Gives me an empty-eyed smile like a good Candor girl. She can play at it when she wants.

She just doesn't want to very often. But I guess she doesn't really understand how important it is to hide.

If I explained that, I'd have to explain other things. The things I want to keep a secret.

"Screw math, huh? I've heard of that. They use it for construction, right?" I ask.

"I better learn it, then. I won't be going to college at this rate," Nia says.

"Every student should aim for college." The Message crowds out what I really wanted to say. That it doesn't matter. That her art is more beautiful than anything I'll ever do.

Nia rolls her eyes. "Is it hard being so good?" she asks.

I wish I could tell her the truth. That it's like scratching an itch—with a knife. But the man is sitting there. Besides, I don't tell her everything. If I did, would she still want to be with me?

The man gets up and walks away. I give my rocker a push. It makes a gritty noise against the cement.

"You make it hard to be good," I tell Nia.

She keeps her eyes steady on her drawing. Her hand doesn't stop moving. But the corner of her mouth twitches. I'm forgiven, I think.

Maybe this won't be so hard. She draws. I stare at her. Fit in some extra-credit calc.

I can handle this. I can control it.

The fall sun feels perfect: warm, without the punishment of summer. I slide off my shoes and pull off my socks. Stick my feet out of the shade.

"Wild man," Nia murmurs.

There are kids all over today—getting frozen yogurt, walking to the library, running errands for their parents. A normal day. We fit inside it.

But then I see a blonde head bobbing down the sidewalk. She's stopping at every street pole, leaving a piece of paper hanging on each one.

Mandi has a familiar-looking helper, too: Sherman.

I don't need to see either of them today. It's not that I'm ashamed of being with Nia. And I don't care how it makes Mandi feel.

It's just that Mandi knows me better than most people. She knows the perfect part of me, at least. That means I can't be the real me around her—the person I am with Nia.

It would make Mandi too suspicious.

"I should go." I shove my notebook into my backpack. The music inside stops. It must have hit the off button.

"But there's still daylight. Isn't it against your religion to stop studying before dinner?"

"We didn't study yesterday," I remind her. We went to the woods again. Our playground now. Nobody else's.

"There's not enough of yesterday." Nia pulls my notebook out of the bag. "Do this now so we can do something better tomorrow."

"How come you get to skip your homework?" I ask.

"Because I am the definition of a lost cause." She says it casually. But it has to eat at her. Even with my help—when she'll let me do it—her grades have been bad.

"You're smart, you know," I tell her.

She just stares down at her sketch pad, pencil moving. I'm not sure she even hears me when she's drawing.

Mandi is closer now. I can read the top of her posters: TAG, in big letters across the top.

And then there's Sherman. He follows her to each post. Pulls pieces of tape from a brown roll and hands them to her when she gestures.

He never takes his eyes off her.

I can't leave when she's so close. She'd see, for sure. Besides, I want to know what Sherman is doing to her. With her, I mean.

Is it really what it looks like?

Mandi holds out her hand without looking. Sherman puts tape in it. She tosses her head, ponytail swinging. Says something. Probably telling him he makes the tape balls in the wrong shape.

Both hands drop to his side. He doesn't stop staring at her, but his whole body sags.

Sherman looks different these days. Pressed khakis. Polo shirts. A buzz cut. If the outside means anything, he's changed completely.

But he avoids me. Crashes through the hall like a scared hippo when I see him at school. I thought he was embarrassed or scared.

But now I wonder if he was avoiding me because of Mandi.

Another pole—the closest one to us, now. He gives her another tape ball.

Then she rewards him. Turns around and gives him that bright shiny smile. The one she used to save for me.

Sherman's cheeks turn pink. He licks his lips.

"Oscar?" Mandi switches off the laser-beam smile.

Nia turns to look.

"It's Mandi," I say. Like she doesn't know.

"Is it too late for the dining room?" Nia mutters.

Sherman is whispering something to Mandi. She shakes her head. Then she cocks her finger to him—come—and strides over to us.

"They're coming over," I say. Like I'm the voice-over guy. Not the poor sucker living this moment.

"Does she taste like bubble gum? Or just look like it?" Nia asks. She rests one elbow on the chair arm and drops her chin in her hand.

Finally I think of something right to say. "You taste like SweeTarts."

A slow smile curves Nia's lips. It's still there when they reach our chairs.

"It's good that you're here." Mandi holds out one of the posters.

Sherman tries to give her a piece of tape.

"It's for them," Mandi says through clenched teeth. "Drop the tape. Please."

The whole roll of tape thunks to the ground. But Sherman doesn't look hurt. He's staring at her like she's a brand-new jumbo pack of Tasty Kakes. So delicious she must be a hallucination.

Mandi rattles the poster. "Our first meeting is Tuesday."

Nia takes it. "I needed some scrap paper."

Mandi's eyes wince, like she's been pinched. "It's important to keep our community beautiful."

Sherman nods. "That's right. Graffiti is wrong."

Nia lets out a low laugh. "Oscar worries all the time about graffiti."

Not funny, I want to tell her. She knows all the ways to torture me. Sometimes it doesn't feel good.

"Right, Oscar?" Nia asks. I ignore her and all the Messages fighting to flood my mouth.

"How are you feeling, Sherman?" I ask. "You seem different."

His eyes shoot to Mandi. "She likes me and it's okay. I'm just lucky, is all."

"Is he high or something?" Nia asks.

Sherman is horrified. "Drugs are wrong. Always treat your body with respect."

"Maybe you should try getting high." Nia winks.

"You're rude." Mandi straightens even taller. Then she looks at me. "She's rude."

Nia's looking at me, too. Expecting something, like Mandi. Both of them expecting me to be the Oscar they know.

I remember the day when Nia drew me on the lawn. It felt like Mandi won then. But things are different now.

"Nia's my girlfriend," I say.

Mandi grabs Sherman's elbow. "Sherman Golub is my boyfriend. Sherman Golub makes me happy."

Sherman swallows hard. His eyes meet mine for just a second. He looks guilty, or maybe just nervous. But then he's back to looking at Mandi like he just found her under the Christmas tree.

"I guess we're all big winners." Nia crumples the poster and tosses it on the ground.

I go for it without even thinking. It's in my hand a split second before Mandi's nails scrape the pavement. Reaching for the same thing.

Mandi's fingers brush mine. She pulls back like I'm oozing acid. "Everyone wins when things are tidy."

Nia's look tells me I screwed up.

But in my head, I hear the Message Mandi said. Part of me thinks she's right. I can't help it.

Even if it makes Nia love me less.

chapter 17

IT'S BEEN RAINING for days. The woods are filled with puddles.
The puddles are filled with slimy slithering things.

The woods are off-limits, for now.

But neither of us wants to wait for things to dry out. So tonight
we'll meet at the shed.

It's late. Time for good boys and girls to brush their teeth and put
on their jammies. I take the usual precautions and sneak out.

Her taste is already in my mouth. I want her to touch me. Press
her body into mine and trail her fingers down my back.

But it's not just that. I want to be with someone who knows who
I really am. And still loves me.

When I get close, I can tell something is wrong. Light shows
through the gaps in the picket fence, where it should be dark. Rock
music is playing. I know the song. It's from my secret stash.

Not even Nia has the key. Someone broke in.

I close the gate silently and creep close. The door to the shed is
wide open. It's easy to slide behind it and listen.

There's a loud belch.

"You're a disgusting slob." A girl's voice, laughing. Slurred.

Is it Nia? I'm not sure. Why would she be here with someone else?

Did she forget it's our night? Isn't *every* night our night?

"I'm a big fat evil slob. No way she'd ever want me for real. Not like she wanted Oscar." It's a familiar whine. Sherman.

I wish the pigs had got him.

"Maybe she just likes tall boys. You're almost as tall as Oscar," the girl says. Yes, Nia. It's her. But I can't believe it. Did she invite him here? Or find him here?

Either way she's with him now. It makes me sick to my stomach.

"I'm not exactly an upgrade," Sherman says. "Nobody's as good as Oscar. It's impossible."

I risk a peek through the crack between the door hinges.

There's Sherman, sitting with his back against the potting sink, legs spread wide. He's holding a bottle of my best stuff. And Nia. Sitting far away. Holding a red cup in her long, beautiful fingers. Betrayer fingers.

"Oscar's better than perfect." Sherman taps his finger against his temple. "He's in control, unlike everybody else around here. Buncha brainwashed babies."

"Enough with the brainwashing talk." Nia's voice is loud. She jumps to her feet.

I pull back. I don't want her seeing me, not yet.

Heavy walking noise—she must be wearing her boots. "Let me tell you something," she says. "There's no such thing as secret M-M-Messages. Nobody is being brainwashed."

That's the Message I've been feeding to her, word for word.

"Mandi doesn't like me for my looks. Or my personality." He lets a huge fart rip.

Nia finds it hysterical. "Do you do that in front of her?"

"Can you keep a secret?"

"It's my specialty," she promises. It makes me wonder what I don't know. I take another look and see her settling on the floor again, closer to Sherman.

"I asked for Oscar's girlfriend. I made my parents do it." His voice is softer now. Sad.

"I'm supposed to believe Mommy and Daddy gave you a girl-friend?" She laughs. "Did they pay extra for the blonde model with inflatable boobs?"

"I ran away—did Oscar tell you?" Sherman asks.

"No. I didn't even know you guys were friends."

"Good friends. *Best* friends," Sherman says. "We had a special relationship."

I almost leap into the shed to throttle him. But I suck in a deep breath. Listen and learn, Oscar. Make him pay later.

"Well, you must be best friends if you know about this place," Nia says.

She doesn't know about my clients. That plenty of kids have seen my secrets in the shed. But all of them are gone. Nobody can tell. Except Sherman.

"He probably hates me now. I thought I hated him, too, but—not anymore." Sherman sighs, a big gusty sound. "I need him to help me."

"You're losing me," Nia says.

"We need more to drink. Gimme." There's a glugging sound. More good stuff pouring into their plastic cups.

"Slow down, that's his favorite," Nia says.

"He won't mind sharing with his girl and his former best friend," Sherman says.

He swallows so loudly, I can hear it. Then he keeps blabbing. "I was supposed to get extra brainwashing after I ran away. But my parents said no. They said it was *their* fault I wasn't happy. They said they hadn't worked hard enough on our relationship."

"So you asked for a pony?" Nia teases.

"No. They told me all about the Messages, even though they weren't supposed to tell anyone. He made them promise when we moved here."

"Who?"

"Oscar's dad. He runs the show."

"He's just the guy who makes sure everyone mows their lawns."

Sherman snorts. "He's in charge of everything and everyone. Which is how he made it happen. Mommy told me I could have anything I wanted if I'd stay in Candor. So . . . I picked a person."

"Mandi." Nia isn't laughing anymore. "You asked them to *give* you Mandi?"

Sherman didn't get lucky. Mandi got brainwashed.

She's not my girlfriend anymore. I never loved her like I love Nia. But it still makes me sick. Does Dad have any limits? Does Sherman?

Who should I hate more? The one who asked for it? Or the one who gave it to him?

"I'm not proud. But it's not my fault. Oscar's so perfect. I just wanted to be like him."

"Next time try ironing your shirts instead," Nia says. I can't tell what she's thinking. Is she disgusted? Angry? Convinced he's crazy?

But no matter how she feels, she's listening. I have to stop this before he convinces her that the Messages are real.

Or maybe I should fix things for good. Call Dad. Tell him Sherman's run away again—and I know exactly where he is.

The white van would pick him up. No windows. Candor crest painted on each side. The Messages would bombard him from the minute they strapped him to the bench.

He wouldn't escape the Listening Room this time. Dad would insist. Everything would be wiped away.

But then they might take Nia, too.

I'll do anything to keep things the way they are now.

I take a step closer and the grass crunches. No, it's glass, from the window next to the door. Now I know how he got in. Nia didn't set this up.

Sherman shoved his way into our secrets. This is all his fault.

I walk inside and go straight to Sherman. I grab the bottle from his hand. "Get your own hooch. And your own girl."

Sherman's eyes are big. He scrabbles backward with his feet, like a dying bug. "Don't be mad," he gasps. "I swear I'll pay for the window."

"Just get out."

"But I need your help," he says.

"I'm done with that."

"I didn't even know you were friends," Nia says behind us.

"We're not."

"We kind of broke up." Sherman hangs his head.

"We were never friends."

"Seems like he knows you pretty well," Nia says. "For someone who was never your friend."

"You need to go. Now," I tell Sherman.

Sherman reaches for the bottle, but I step back. His empty hand flaps on the ground. "I was his most treasured client. I guess that's you now."

"Nia's my girlfriend. Not my client," I say.

He rips out another belch. "Whatever you say."

"Get up." I grab his wrist and give a hard yank. He staggers to his feet.

"Let him stay," Nia says. "I'm learning so much."

I don't like the tone of her voice. It's suspicious. Maybe a little angry.

"Give me just one more CD," Sherman pleads.

"You give him CDs, too?" Nia asks.

I can't do anything except lie. "Of course not."

"You better listen to them, art girl," Sherman says. "Or you'll never get out."

Nia looks confused. Which is how I want things to stay.

Sherman squeezes his eyes shut like he's in pain. "Make me forget, Oscar."

Interesting. For once we want the same thing.

"Make me like the rest of them. Take away everything else," he says.

This could solve my problems. But I can't make a deal in front of Nia. "Come on. I'll walk you home."

"Okay, pal." Sherman swings one arm around my shoulders. "But promise me. Promise you'll make me forget why she wants me. You can do that."

First he makes Mandi like him. Then he wants to believe it's true. He doesn't deserve my help.

I shove his arm off me. "We have nothing to talk about."

"Like you're so perfect?" Sherman tilts his head toward Nia. "Is she strictly voluntary?"

"What's he mean?" Nia asks. But slowly, like she's already figuring it out.

"Shut up," I warn Sherman. "Or I'll tell my dad you want a trip to the Room."

"My parents won't send me there." Sherman's face is smug. "They're afraid of the side effects."

They *should* be afraid. He knows too much. It could take days to wipe his brain clean. That's longer than anyone is supposed to be in there.

Bad things happen when you skip the Messages. But bad things also happen when you get too many of them.

Nothing as bad as what I'm going to do to Sherman if he doesn't shut it.

"Leave *now*," I growl.

"No." Nia's shout fills the room. "Tell me more, Sherman. Tell me about . . ." She tries to say it. But she can't. "Those things. You know."

Sherman shoves past me and crouches at her feet. "You ever wonder why you want bran instead of Pop-Tarts? Why you floss every single night?"

"Everyone likes bran," I say. But they both ignore me.

"I bet you wanted dry rye toast and egg whites for breakfast this morning," Sherman whispers.

Nia's eyes go big.

"Everybody loves rye toast, too," I say. I try to catch her eye. I shake my head: *Sherman's crazy. Don't listen.*

But her eyes are locked on his.

Nia holds up her hand and shows him her fingernails. Perfect little ovals polished in pink. "Why did black seem so ugly all of a sudden?"

"They control everything. Everything that's in your head, they put there." Sherman is so calm now. In control. Like he sweated all the whiskey onto the shed floor.

"Don't let him scare you. It's just stupid stories." I kneel on the floor next to Nia. But she slides away.

"This man can fix it." Sherman aims a chubby finger at me.

"There's nothing to fix," I tell Nia.

Sherman holds the same fat finger to his lips. "Shh. It's a secret."

"Tell me about Oscar," Nia says. "How does he fix things?"

"Those CDs keep your head clear." He taps his head. "Oscar's good brainwashing keeps away the bad brainwashing."

A bead of sweat rolls down my head and slides into my ear.

Nia takes in a deep breath. Holds it for a second, then exhales. Crosses her arm. "Let me see if I've got this right. This town screws with your mind."

"Yes."

"And it made Mandi like you."

Sherman stares at his feet. But he nods.

She keeps going. "And Oscar twists your mind, too—"

"I don't," I interrupt.

"It's not really *twisting*," Sherman says. "Oscar's helping you. Probably."

"I don't need that kind of help." Nia stands up and staggers against the cabinets. I'm up, next to her, balancing her. But she jerks away.

"It's just a story. You know there's no such thing as Messages," I tell her.

Nia backs toward the door, holding both hands in front of her like a shield. "Every single kid ordered the baby carrots at lunch yesterday."

"Who doesn't love baby carrots?"

"I'm not listening to your CDs anymore," she says.

"No. You have to."

"Why?"

"Because . . ." There's no way to say it without making her mad. But I have to make sure she keeps listening. "Because they're special."

Her face is stone. "Then it's true."

"Sort of . . ."

"Tell me the truth." Her voice is low. Each word is like her pencil jabbing paper. Pointed and hard.

"Fine. It's all true."

She takes a step back and shakes her head. Her eyes are wide.

"How do I know?" she whispers.

"Know what?"

"How do I know I love you?"

"That part's real. No Messages. I never made you love me." I reach out for her. "I'm not Sherman."

She steps away. "You're lying."

I gave you the real me, I want to say. *And you loved me.* "I was only trying to help you."

"Like I said," Sherman pipes in. "He's a giver."

"I'm done with your help." She runs out the door. I follow her. Her hand is on the gate handle.

"Don't be stupid. You need me. You need that music," I say.

"Maybe you need me," Nia says. "But I never needed you."

The gate snaps shut behind her. Before I can open it again, there's the thunk of her skateboard wheels. There's no catching her now.

I can hear him behind me. Gulping in more oxygen than he deserves. Sherman takes all kinds of things he shouldn't.

"Maybe you should have told her the truth," he says.

My fists form into rocks. I launch my body into his. He's down. I'm over him. In control.

Sherman's eyes are wet and weak. Begging to be hit.

I imagine it. A punch into the middle of his flabby stomach first. When I was done with my hands, I'd use my feet.

The Messages boil in my brain.

Never harm another person.
Violence is never acceptable.
Don't hit.

The heat floods me. Relaxes every muscle. I can't fight it. I'm floating in it, swirling, pulled into the middle.

"Violence is never acceptable," Sherman croaks.

"You deserve it," I whisper.

"I know." He squeezes his eyes shut. Nods.

But the Messages push me off him. I fall into the wet grass. Feel the water seep into my pants.

"Why do you ruin everything?" I ask.

Sherman curls into a ball. "I'm sorry," he says.

It makes me hate him even more.

"I'm the one who's sorry," I say. Sorry I didn't give him what he deserved.

Not tonight.

But another time, I'll find a way.

chapter 18

IF MY LIFE were a movie, I'd go to her house. Climb in her window and make her listen. Show her I love her and she loves me.

But it's past midnight. Already most of my excuses for being home late won't work. And even though Nia hurt me, Dad could do worse.

So I go home. Lay in bed and practice what I'll say. Now that she knows about my special Messages, I know I did something wrong. I have to explain.

"I never made you love me," I whisper to the glowing stars on my ceiling. "I just protected you."

I don't remember when my mouth got quiet or when my eyes closed. But when I wake up the next morning, I'm ready. I'm going to find her and fix things.

I get to school early. Wait outside the doors. I think I promise to take notes at the next traffic safety club. I'm not sure. It's hard to focus.

Mandi gets there before Nia. The wrong girl in the wrong place. Her eyes are red and her nose is puffy-pink.

Part of me wants to tell her: *You don't really want Sherman. Just walk away.*

But it's too risky. Besides, she wouldn't believe me.

"Sherman was attacked," she says. Her mouth pulls into a tight, straight line.

"Really?" I almost laugh. Then I remember she's serious. I give her wide, worried eyes. "That's horrible. Who did it?"

"He says he doesn't remember anything." Mandi swallows hard. "But he looks dreadful. His face is covered in scratches and he has a black eye. I think some outsider kids must have jumped him."

That's what stealing a bottle of my finest hooch will do to you. Kid probably staggered into hibiscus bushes and plastic fences all the way home. I could have smacked him senseless and he never would have remembered. I wish I'd ignored the Messages. I wish I was strong enough to do what I want all the time.

Especially if I wasn't caught.

"I hope he's better soon," I tell her.

"Oh, he *will* be." She says it like she's in control of his body.

I'm not the only one who's used to things going their way.

Then a cold, thin hand grabs mine. Tugs.

It's Nia, all in black. She stares at me, then tilts her head. Away from school.

The bell rings.

"Aren't you coming?" Mandi looks at both of us.

"In a minute. Don't wait," I say.

She goes.

We stand there, rocks in a stream, kids flowing around us. I can't get my feet to walk away from school. But I won't leave her, either.

"Now or never," Nia says in a flat voice.

It unsticks my feet. I follow her, away from school. With no excuses to make. No way to save us if somebody stops us.

But nobody does. She drops my hand after a minute, giving hers a shake like it's covered in something disgusting. And then she leads me to the fountain.

The fountain is across from the movie theater, on a special platform overlooking the lake. It's made to play in. You just walk onto it—it's a big circle next to the sidewalk—and wait for the water to come. It spurts out of the ground, different jets at different times.

"Maybe we should go to the woods," I say.

"I don't care if you're safe."

"I care if you are," I say.

She sits on a bench overlooking the fountain. The only thing behind her is a railing and the lake.

I think through what I practiced last night. Where to start.

"I never made you do anything," I say.

"You messed with my head." She won't look at me. Just watches the water.

"Only to protect you. To stop the Messages from doing things you shouldn't."

"Like ratting you out." A smile twitches her lips back, but it's gone fast.

"Maybe at first. But then—then I didn't want you to change."

The fountain water is receding. The jets die, and all that's left are low bubbles. But there's still the sound of water, rushing into the drain.

"I would never rat you out," she says softly.

"You wouldn't mean to. But the Messages can make you do anything."

"Including love you?"

"You still love me?" A swirl of happy and desperate fills my chest.

"I don't love you." She shakes her head. "Not anymore. I make my own decisions now."

Now is the time to tell her: *I love you. I want you. I would never hurt you.*

It might be my only chance.

But I'm angry. She really thinks I made her love me. Like I'm Sherman. The rebel part of her must hate wanting me. So this is her excuse: there was really no choice at all.

"Nobody made you want me," I tell her.

"I'll never believe you." Her voice is low. She still won't look at me.

This isn't how I planned things. I don't know how to get back on track. Stupid words come out of my mouth. "I could have any girl I want. Without the Messages."

"Not me. Not anymore." Nia stands up.

So do I. I step close. She wavers. But doesn't move.

"I'll do anything," I say. "Just don't leave me." Worse than stupid: pathetic.

Her eyes are a green shield. I can't see what's inside. I grab both her wrists.

She tries to pull away, but I won't let go. I am stronger than that. "You want to be like the rest of them? All SATs and grades and being perfect? You want to become Mandi?"

She rolls her eyes and laughs. It's a bitter, small sound. "She was good enough for two years, wasn't she? Or did she not have a say in that, either? Do you rape all your girlfriends' minds?"

Rape.

I drop her wrists. Since when did I have to force anything with a girl?

"I'm done," I say. No more chasing and begging and *feeling.*

"So am I." But she doesn't go anywhere. Just stands there, staring at me with her mirror eyes and that mouth that said something so ugly, I'll never forget.

She's not worth saving.

"Nobody tells me what to do," she says.

I laugh, louder than the fountain. Loud enough to make people stare.

I don't care.

"Throw away my CDs," I tell her. "Then you'll see who's controlling you."

"I will." She whispers it. Even looks hurt. "I already stopped listening."

Maybe I'd have a chance, if I said the right thing right now.

But I'm done.

"It'll only take a few days, and then you'll be gone," I tell her.

"You're wrong," Nia says. "I'm too strong for that."

"Maybe it'll be a week. Even two. But after that"—I snap my fingers—"I'll be the only real one left."

"You and your dad," she says.

"Yeah. Me and my dad." It hurts, being lumped in with him. But she's right. Soon we'll be the only two people in town who think for themselves.

That's her fault. Not mine.

"See you." My feet know where to go: back to school. I take a step away from her. Another. I want to go where I can obey the Messages for the rest of the day. Ignore the hurt boiling inside me.

But she's not done yet. "Good luck with the next girl. Maybe she'll be a redhead. You can round out the trifecta."

"Or maybe she'll be smart." I know how to hurt her, too.

I just never wanted to before.

Her eyes are shiny with tears, but her mouth is small and hard. And silent.

"I'd say you'll be sorry, but soon you won't even remember this,"

I say. Then I let the Messages take me where I'm supposed to be.
Toward school. Away from her.

Back to how I'm supposed to live my life.

Safe.

And alone.

chapter 19

WHEN THE DOORBELL rings at six A.M., I think it has to be Nia. Sorry for what she said. Wanting me back. She'll say she understands what I did.

Maybe I'll listen.

I'm at the door before Dad can set his coffee cup down.

But it's not Nia. It's Mandi, wearing a T-shirt that says TAG PA-TROL. Her perma-perky smile is missing and she's tapping her toe.

"Get your father," she says. "He has to come see."

"See what? The sun isn't even up."

She sighs and looks around me. "Where is he? I mean . . . please."

"Dad!" I shout it. I'm too tired to be polite. I stayed at the shed until midnight, looking at pictures of paintings and ODing on M&M's. Forgetting her isn't as easy as walking away.

Dad's loafers click on the wood floor. I smell coffee behind me.

"It's Mandi," I say unnecessarily.

He steps next to me so we form a solid Banks man-wall. "I thought you two broke up."

"This goes beyond romance." Mandi folds her arms. "There's more graffiti. We found it on patrol."

"What color?" I ask.

It wasn't me. But was it her? Really, who else could it have been?

Dad and Mandi both give me surprised looks. I asked the wrong question.

But Mandi answers anyway. "Orange," she snaps.

"More coffee." Dad holds out his cup. "In a travel mug."

I get it. And follow him into her candy-pink NEV, not asking if it's okay. She drives toward downtown. Dad takes the jump seat and spends the ride calming Mandi down.

"Graffiti is a blight on our town," he says. "And it will be dealt with as such."

"I hope you're right. Because it's important to keep our town beautiful," she tells him.

I love when Dad's Messages bite him in the butt.

But I'm not feeling any joy this morning. It's more like fear mixed with a touch of déjà vu. Because I know only one person in Candor who likes collecting cans of orange spray paint. Someone who's pissed. Who thinks she has nothing to lose by spreading a little blight around.

She's so wrong.

Mandi pulls up in front of the fountain.

The words are in a perfect circle around the center of the fountain. *BETTER COVER YOUR EARS.*

It's not just graffiti. It's graffiti that says, *Na-na-na-na-boo-boo, I know the secret.* Why go halfway? Why not royally screw yourself?

The sun isn't even up, but there's already a group of about twenty people standing around. They're in small clumps, murmuring, staring. But nobody comes up to us. They just talk louder so we can hear them.

"It's just awful," one old woman says. She's got a little white dog on a leash.

Her fat bald buddy slurps coffee from a silver Candor mug. "Classic gang activity. I know all the signs."

Dad lifts his walkie-talkie to his mouth. "Why hasn't this been taken care of?" he barks.

Static. Then Bart, sounding scared. "Good morning, sir."

"Hardly," Dad spits.

"We're halfway through," the voice says. "But there's some kind of shellac on top."

"Did you take a coffee break? You're not here." Dad manages to smile at the crowd. Everyone's watching him, wanting him to make it better.

Now Bart speaks slowly. "Mr. Banks. Where are you?"

"The fountain."

"We're at the welcome sign."

Mandi's eyes get big. "Let's go."

The welcome sign isn't your typical "Population 6,230" sign. It's some ankle biter's art, blown up to sign size. It's a drawing of people walking a dog—or maybe a bobcat; it's hard to say for sure. The sign reads, DRIVE SLOW, CHILDREN AT PLAY.

When we get there, four men in Candor polos are scrubbing the sign. The crowd is even bigger here.

"What's it say?" Dad growls.

The men stand back.

YOU ARE WHAT YOU HEAR.

He touches it with his thumb. Shakes his head. "We'll fix this," he says.

"When will it be gone?" somebody shouts from the crowd.

Dad looks at the crowd and says it louder. "We'll fix this."

I don't think he's talking about the spray paint.

The worker guys are arguing about something. Two are shaking their heads. One has his arms crossed, staring at his feet. The brave one looks at Dad.

"Chris just radioed from the flagpole," he says. "There's more."

"Not the bricks." Dad strides to Mandi's NEV and waits for us to catch up. His arm snakes up to touch the roof of the NEV. His fingers are drumming against it all the way to the flagpole.

Mandi actually goes three miles over the speed limit.

The crowd is standing in a circle around the flagpole, three people deep. You'd think there wouldn't be room for us. But when people see it's Dad, they step back and forward and to the side until we have a prime viewing spot.

The letters are in a precise checkerboard pattern across the bricks.

YOU ARE NOT IN CHARGE.

Two polo shirt guys are on their knees, scrubbing. Everyone else watches them and whispers.

They stop when Dad's shiny shoes get close. "Tell me it's coming off."

"We tried everything," one says. "Except sandblasting."

"Or taking them out," the other mutters.

Dad stands up tall and puts his hands on his hips. "Whoever did this," he says loudly, "will pay."

And then he gets down on his knees. "Get me a crowbar," he says.

Someone gasps in the crowd.

Crowbar guy double-times it.

Dad sticks the curved end under the brick with the Y on it. It's six years old. *HOLMES FAMILY. FINALLY AT HOME!* it reads.

"Good choice," I mutter.

Mandi takes time off from grimacing righteously to give me a suspicious look. "What did you say?"

"It's devastating, et cetera," I tell her.

"Excuse me, please. I think I know who did this," Mandi says loudly.

The crowd goes quiet. Dad's crowbar freezes.

"I know, too," I say. Because there's someone else who deserves to be hurt. Someone who ruined more than a few bricks. Someone I need to fix, permanently.

And I still want to protect her.

Mandi stares straight at me when she says it. "It was Nia Silva."

I answer her fast. "No way. It was Sherman Golub."

We both look at Dad. He presses his lips together and nods grimly. "Kids," he says, "I think you're both right."

chapter **20**

WE GO TO school like it's any other day.

There was no choice. It was almost seven. The Messages make sure every good girl and boy is headed for first period.

And as King Good Boy, how could I do anything different?

I looked for her everywhere. Study hall. Lunch. Founder's Park.

But Nia doesn't come to school. Neither does Sherman. It should be good news that he's not here. But I can't be happy. If both are missing, they probably went to the same place.

The Listening Room.

All I can do is wait. I wait through school and dinner and dishes and three hours of staring at the same page of my chem book.

Still the light under my father's door is on. It's nearly midnight. Isn't he going to go to bed? Let him go to bed. I don't want him leaving. Not tonight.

But then I hear the door alarm squeal. He's left. And that means Nia might not be safe. There's only one place he'd go at this hour.

I wait fifteen minutes. Stuff the bed with pillows and wet my toothbrush. Just in case he beats me home.

Then I walk downtown, staying in any shadows I can find.

Dad built the Listening Room after Mom left. Maybe he thought he could have kept her if he'd put her there. Or maybe he was hoping to find her. Bring her back.

Then he could have made her love us enough to stay.

It doesn't look like a place where people's every independent thought is erased. You'd expect it to be hidden away, in a warehouse on the edge of town or in a basement. But Candor doesn't have warehouses (too ugly) or basements (we're built on top of a swamp; they'd flood), and Dad thinks the Listening Room is just swell. Why hide away one of his most genius inventions?

So it's on Candor Avenue, the road that cuts through the heart of town. There's a row of little shops—dog bakery, picture-framing place, a realtor's office—and then the Listening Room. Frosted glass door. Gold letters on the front:

CANDOR SPA. BY APPOINTMENT ONLY.

Nobody goes there for pedicures.

It's not hidden, but it's discreet. Kids don't know about it. Neither do our visitors. Dad tells people about it only after they've moved in and something isn't right. Can't quit smoking in a week? Come for a few hours. Drug habit? Maybe an overnight would be best.

I go to the alley behind the shops. His NEV is parked there.

I hurry up the fire stairs to the roof. One easy pull-up and I'm on the clay roof tiles.

The smart thing would be to go home. I'm supposed to be done with her. That's what I told her. The Room can fix the rest.

But I can't go home. I thought all I'd ever remember are the horrible things she said. But all I can think about are the good parts. Black toenails under blue water. Laughing at the pathetic clones we were so different from. How she tasted like vanilla. All I remember are the things I miss. And that she loved me.

There are dormer windows tucked in along the slope of the roof.

I belly-crawl until I can see the fronts of the windows. There are four. Two are lit up.

Just enough for Sherman and Nia.

I ease over to the first one. It's not hard. The roof is nearly flat, with ridged clay tiles that give me something to hold on to.

I peer inside.

It looks like a five-star hotel room. Big bed with a million fluffy pillows. An enormous chair with a blanket draped over one arm. But the walls don't have any pictures on them, and there isn't a TV. Everything is white.

You can't see the speakers. There are thirty of them. Behind the walls. In the ceiling. Under the rug. It's impossible to touch them. Or to stop the music that's playing.

Someone is lying on the bed facedown. T-shirt stretched tight over back blubber. Khakis slipping down his butt. Greasy hair that's probably leaving a mark on that snow-white pillow.

Beautiful. It's Sherman.

He has his hands over his ears. His body is still. I wonder if he's trying to fight it.

This is exactly what I needed to happen. And it's what he deserves. Sherman will be erased. Molded into a nice Candor boy. There won't be any room in his brain to remember me. And he definitely won't feel like making any kind of mischief.

I can't feel happy, even though this is what I wanted. More than that: it's what I made happen. But it means that maybe Mandi got what she wanted, too.

Until I check the other window, the only thing I'll feel is terror. Please let it be a housewife who can't stop eating. Or a chain-smoker workaholic asshole. Somebody, anybody, except Nia.

I see headlights coming down the street. Somebody's out late.

I flatten my body against the roof and hold on to the tile tight.

Then I hear the hum. It's the mosquito truck. A white cloud follows behind it: harmless orange citrus spray, Dad tells people. The finest in pest control.

He doesn't mention the Messages that play from speakers hidden in the roof. Whenever everybody needs to forget something, Dad sends out the truck. It drives all night long. The brain is most receptive at night.

I brought my iPod, just in case. I pull the earphones out of my front pocket and jam them in my ears. Hit play.

These are my emergency Messages. They keep me strong when the truck is out. Or when I feel myself slipping.

I close my eyes as it goes by.

"The Messages don't own me," I mutter. "I control my own thoughts."

Nothing floods my brain. But I wonder what it was. Something about forgetting the graffiti, I bet. Maybe even something about Sherman.

Or Nia.

The truck is gone. I slither to the other lit window.

Nia. Sitting on the edge of her chair, with her head in her hands. She's rocking. Rocking, like a crazy monkey in a zoo.

"No." I slam my fist on the tile. It makes a useless thud. She won't hear it. She wouldn't hear me if I shouted at the top of my lungs. The music is loud inside. And there's never a break.

Still I try. I bang on the window. But she doesn't look up.

Just keeps rocking.

What would I do, anyway? What if she looked up and saw me here?

A long time ago, I found Dad's folders about the Listening Room. They filled an entire drawer in his office at home. Blueprints. Papers about extreme brainwashing—"mind control," they called it. Case studies. And a long list of side effects.

It's bad enough that he's erasing her. But what comes after will be worse. Migraines. Amnesia. Tremors. Cravings to eat things that aren't food. Usually those fade away in a few weeks. But a few people have it worse. Strokes. Psychosis. An uncontrollable urge to hurt yourself.

I study the blueprints every few weeks, to see if I'm missing something. A way out. Just in case. I haven't found it yet.

"Fight it." I say it like she can hear me. I spread my hand against the window. Slices of white room glow between each finger.

She's pacing now. How long will it take before she gives in?

I remember how her lips felt on mine. How she stared at me. And then she drew the real me, right on a flat piece of paper.

And now I'm losing her. It's all being wiped away. Everything special. Maybe—probably—her memories of us.

I shouldn't have walked away. I shouldn't have said I was done.

I should have begged her to understand. Made her listen until she wasn't mad, mad enough to do something stupid.

Something that would guarantee we'd never be together.

Then I find the right words to say. If I'd told her this, maybe things would be different. It's too late. But I say it anyway.

"I'm sorry," I whisper. "I love you."

She pauses for a second and tugs at her hair. Like she heard me.

I know she didn't. But I can't leave, not yet. I'll stay with her until sunrise. If I brace my feet, I won't slide. I can rest my cheek on the roof tile and still see her. Pacing. Pulling her hair.

"I'll fix you," I tell her. "I promise."

Even though I don't know how.

It's better than good-bye.

chapter 21

DAD SENDS ME grocery shopping on Saturday morning. Like it's a normal week. Like before. Before I loved Nia. Before he ruined her.

"If they don't have skim, skip it. And don't forget: organic." Dad slaps the grocery list in my hand, along with some cash.

He doesn't bother telling me to give him the change back. In his mind I'm still perfect. I'm not a kid who sneaks out every night and crawls onto the roof of the Listening Room. Watches his girl get slowly erased.

He doesn't even notice my bloodshot eyes.

It's been four nights. Nia isn't pacing anymore. She's sitting, mostly. Last night she took an hour to brush her hair before she went to sleep.

Sleep. She didn't do that the first three nights. Does that mean she's nearly broken? Nobody stays strong forever in the Listening Room.

Even I would break eventually.

"Why don't you pick up some frozen yogurt? A special treat," he says. Dad's been in a great mood since he sent Nia and Sherman to the Listening Room.

"You're the best," I say. It's easiest to act grateful, even if I hate him. Without sleep it's hard to fight all the time.

McKennon's is grocery-store porn. The produce is stacked in glistening pyramids. It always smells like fresh-baked bread, even by the fish counter. The cans and boxes are on shallow wood shelves. Nothing is too high or deep. There's always jazz music playing.

As usual it's full of ponytail mommies in yoga pants with shiny-faced babies. One of them gives me an approving smile.

"Cookie!" The kid holds up a carrot with the feathery green still attached to the top.

"Seriously?" I ask.

The woman gives me a wide-eyed *don't say anything* look and walks away fast. I watch her go. Yoga pants are the tightest pants you see in Candor.

If I'm fast, I can drive the NEV past Nia's house when I'm done. See if there's any sign. I'm not sure what to look for. But maybe something will show me how she's doing since last night. When she'll come home.

Besides, I like seeing the curtains in her window. I pretend she's inside, drawing, or chewing on her black nail polish.

Aisle 7, canned fruits. I grab the biggest jar of unsweetened applesauce. Dad's favorite snack. The jar is so clean, my fingers squeak against it.

Another cart rolls up next to me. At first I don't pay any attention. But the cart doesn't keep going. My neck burns like I'm being stared at.

I slide my eyes sideways. There's a girl my age. She's standing completely still. Like I'm a wild animal and she doesn't want to scare me. Her eyes are fastened to my face.

"There's plenty." I move forward. "Help yourself."

"I can't believe you shop here," she says. "Oscar Banks shops in the same store as my family. We buy food from the same shelves."

Great. A groupie. "It's the only grocery store in Candor," I tell her.

"I'm so silly. I forget things lately." She rubs her head and for a second her smile dims, like something hurts.

The girl looks different when she doesn't have a psycho smile stretched across her face. She's still all Candor: clothes two sizes too big, white sneakers, ponytail. But now she looks familiar. It makes me feel good, somehow.

"Are you in one of my classes?" I ask. "Math, maybe?"

She shakes her head, and I get a whiff of baby powder. "We're in the same lunch. I've seen you sitting with your pretty girlfriend and all those really smart kids."

"You mean Nia?" Saying her name to somebody else feels good. Like she still exists.

She squints at me. "What?"

"My girlfriend. Her name is Nia."

"That's weird." Her smile is sickeningly fast and sweet—almost robotic. "My name is Nia."

My hand opens up and there's a loud pop. I feel something wet against my foot.

"Your applesauce!" She shoves her cart away and bends low to look at my foot.

I look down at the top of her head. Dark brown hair. Little ears with holes running down their curves. Earrings used to be in there.

"You're Nia Silva?" I have to force the words over my teeth.

"You *do* know me!" She pops back to her feet. "Wow! I feel famous."

Her green eyes look so small without the black ring of mascara and eye goop. Like a child's eyes. They're all wrong. I can barely look at them.

"I know who you are." It comes out as a whisper.

But she doesn't know me. Not who I am to her, at least.

Amnesia is a common side effect. Or maybe all of the Messages they fed her made her want to forget.

They erased *us*.

"You might have glass in your foot." She gives me a sweet, worried smile that I've never seen on her face before. "Maybe you'd better go to the doctor. Let me take you."

"No. I don't need help." It sounds rude. But I can't do it. She's not Nia.

It's disgusting. They melted my girl down and poured her into their mold. And this perversion is what she cooled into. I can't be near her. Can't see her, smell her, hear her voice chirping like a bird.

I tell her the same thing I've been whispering every night on the roof. "I'm sorry. It's my fault."

"Everybody makes mistakes." She shrugs. "They'll clean it up in five minutes."

We both stare at the floor. There's red now. My blood, mixing with the pale yellow of the applesauce.

"I have to go." I fish my foot out of the glop and stagger down the aisle. I have to get away, fast. But everything moves too slowly. I feel like I fell asleep in the meat freezer and woke up in another world. I'm numb, shocked, my brain too sluggish to keep up with what's happening.

My feet won't work right. I stumble into the display at the end of the aisle. Boxes are falling, yellow cereal boxes, blocking my escape.

I walk right over them. My feet smash cardboard, crunching whatever healthy grain yuck is inside. I slip on one box and almost hit the ground. But I'm up and moving faster now. Almost away from her. Away from the place where I learned what I'd lost.

"See you at school, then!" she calls after me.

I make the mistake of looking back. As if the picture would be different now.

It's not.

She bends her arm at the elbow and sticks her hand up, like a beauty queen. Then she wiggles her fingers good-bye.

I don't wave back.

A stock boy is here now. He's stacking the fallen boxes. In a few minutes nobody will know what I did.

Everything will be perfect again.

Except for my life.

chapter 22

AS SOON AS I'm outside, Dad's car pulls up. One tinted window slides down. "The manager called," he says.

I thought I hated him before, but now I know what hate is. I want to get even for what he did. He took away my girl and made her forget everything important. Now all that's left is another useless Candor clone.

But I still have to survive. Alone. So I open the door to get in.

"Wait." Dad holds up a towel. "Is there blood?"

I nod.

He spreads the towel on the plush floor mat. "Okay. Now you can get in."

Nice to know the car comes first. I guess it cost a lot more than me.

Tears leak out of my eyes and slide down my neck. They puddle where the seat belt crosses over my shirt.

"Does it hurt that much?" Dad shoots me a worried look.

"More than you'd think," I tell him.

If he'd known how much I love her, would he have still done it? Should I have begged? Tried harder to save her? I'm his son. Maybe that would have mattered.

Or maybe it would have made things worse.

"We're going to the hospital," he says.

Sick people shouldn't have to leave Candor. That's what all the marketing literature says. And the Messages make sure everyone agrees.

"Let me go home." I sound whiney, like a kid.

"You will go. And you will get better," he says. Gives me a stare that warns me not to argue. "Banks men are strong."

"It's just a cut."

"Maybe it's more." Now he stares straight ahead. Fear pushes away the pain. Where are we really going? What will happen when we get there?

We pull into the ambulance parking, right at the entrance of the hospital. Not the Listening Room. I've never been so happy to see it. Maybe I'm safe.

Dad grabs a wheelchair and points. I get in and he takes me inside.

The waiting room has a vaulted ceiling, with big windows that overlook a lake. The furniture has thick cushions with a palm tree pattern. There aren't any TVs, just soft "healing music" that plays 24/7, everywhere: patient rooms, treatment rooms, even operating rooms.

We go to a desk. It feels like we're opening a bank account, not showing up sick.

I've never been here, unless you count the grand openings for different wings. Candor kids don't break a lot of bones.

"No big deal," I tell the nurse at the desk. "I just need a Band-Aid."

"Fill these out." She slaps a fat packet in front of Dad. "Welcome, Mr. Banks. It's an honor to have you here."

Even town founders have to fill out paperwork. Dad sighs and scribbles his signature on the first page of the packet. Flips. Writes some more. Flips.

It's a lot of writing for a cut foot. I lean close and try to read it.

The glass doors hiss open behind us. The nurse glances over. Her eyes get big.

It's a couple, half-carrying a guy into the ER. He's taller than both of them. His head hangs low, bouncing, swinging, like it's connected by a single elastic thread.

"Ouchies! Ouchies!" he yells in a high voice.

Dad looks, too. But when he sees who it is, he turns half away. Like he doesn't want to be seen. "He shouldn't be here," he mutters.

The kid is fat. Familiar. It has to be Sherman, out from the Listening Room, too.

I can't see his face; his chin is tucked against his chest. A long string of drool slides from his mouth and dangles above the polished tile floor.

"What's wrong with him?" I ask.

"He's fine. Focus on your foot," Dad snaps.

Sure. He looks great. This wouldn't have anything to do with having his brain steam-cleaned for four days.

It's my fault. It ripples through my mind like a Message. But it's my voice. Something my brain cooked up all on its own.

No. It's not my fault. It's my father. He's the one who invented the Messages. The Listening Room. He's the one who locked Sherman and Nia in there.

Dad leans over the desk and whispers something to the nurse.

She picks up her phone and pushes a red button. "Pizza delivery for Dr. Stevens," she says. "Overbaked."

They have codes for this. Like it happens all the time.

"Do you see them?" Sherman lifts his face now. "They're all over! Biting! Biting!"

The other people in the waiting room stop staring at him and look at the ground. "Where? Where are they?" a little girl yells.

Dad makes a frantic gesture. Our nurse rushes away and pushes through double doors. Running away from Dad or running to get help. I don't know which.

The woman with Sherman strokes his cheek with her free hand. Rings sparkle from every finger except her thumb. "There's nothing there, baby." I recognize her now, from the brick ceremony. Sherman's mother.

Dad's half-turned away now, watching Sherman. But keeping still. Like he doesn't want to be seen.

I know how he feels.

"Watch out!" Sherman picks up one foot, then another, like a bear doing an Irish dance.

The man helping Sherman looks up—his father, I bet. He's clearly spotted us; his eyes are stuck on Dad. "You!" he shouts. "You did this."

Dad finds the energy to get over to them. Real fast.

"Drugs kill," Dad says loudly.

Sherman stops dancing. He's pointing at the ceiling now. Following an invisible something with his finger.

Everyone is staring at Sherman again. And Dad. I know they want him to fix this. He's everybody's daddy in Candor. He makes everything all better.

"This isn't drugs," the man spits. He's almost as tall as Sherman, with the same dirty blond hair and thick lips. But lots more wrinkles.

Sherman's mother chimes in. "My baby never did drugs!"

"Look!" Sherman cries, still looking up. "A dead bird!"

"You're embarrassing yourself," Dad murmurs. "Sit down and wait for the doctors."

"You said this would *help* him," Sherman's father says. "And now look at him. I knew we never should have consented to this."

Now Dad lowers his voice and I can't hear him anymore. People look away, sensing this is None of Their Business.

Except for me. I get up and hobble closer. My foot hurts. I picture a trail of blood behind me on the floor, like a slug leaving its trail on the sidewalk. But when I check, there's nothing there.

They don't notice me standing behind Dad. "I didn't approve his release," he says. "He wasn't ready."

"We pulled him out. My wife had a bad feeling, and she was right. My boy's brain is destroyed." Sherman's Dad is getting louder and louder.

"Exercise some discretion." Dad's voice is soft. But clearly in charge.

I've read all of Dad's secret files about the Listening Room. Seen bulleted lists of aftereffects. Pictures. Charts. But I never saw it in person before. It's revolting. Embarrassing. Like I'm watching Sherman dance naked and drunk.

"What's going on?" A short, thin man in blue scrubs steps between Dad and Sherman. He pulls down Sherman's chin so he can look in his eyes.

Sherman's mother points at Dad. "He did it."

The doctor dares to let out a sigh. "Our second one this week."

Dad's lips press together. Then he gives the doctor a tight smile. "I know you'll do your best, Dr. Reeb."

The nurse brings a wheelchair. "Bring him back to the usual room," the doctor tells her.

I step back, over, keep an eye on the nurse. The last thing I want is a surprise ending. Grab Oscar! Bring him back!

The nurse shoves Sherman into the seat with one hand and

straps him in. He yells, "Dead birdie! Dead birdie!"

But now the doctor looks at me. "A third? A real bumper crop."

He pulls a light from his pocket and grabs my chin. I try to jerk away, but the light is in my eyes. Dots everywhere.

"It's just my foot," I say. "No need for you. Or, um, that light."

"How refreshing." The doctor lets go of my face. "He's relatively intact. Sit over there. We'll bring you in. Eventually."

The music in the ceiling switches to a new song. Something with soft flutes, and a violin. It's pretty. I wonder what's underneath.

Will the Messages tell me to forget what happened today?

Or will we just pretend it never happened?

chapter 23

I FIND NIA at lunch. She's sitting at the table of silent studiers, staring at her earth-science book like she used to look at art. Her jaw moves slowly, working on the huge pile of carrots in front of her.

I want her back.

Not the shiny, empty Nia. I want the mouthy, beautiful, sweet-and-sour girl who kissed me. The one who'd still hate me, if she could remember anything besides SAT words and good manners.

Before I get closer, I slide my hand in my pocket. Wrap my fingers around the folded piece of paper I put in there last night, at the shed. A reminder of how things used to be.

My plan. The first part of it, at least.

"Lot of vegetables at this table." I slide into the seat across from her. A girl a few seats down clears her throat and stares at me. I ignore her.

Nia looks up, eyes big. Doesn't get the joke. "Vegetables make you strong. Good food makes good brains." I'll bet if I followed her around for the rest of the day, I could hear half the Messages my dad ever wrote.

"I think I've heard that one before," I say.

"Would you like some?" She pushes the tray toward me.

"Too hard to stomach."

Her eyes narrow, just for a second. "Why are you here?"

It makes me wonder. Does she remember our fight? Any part of *us*?

It's not a question I planned for. I improvise. "You seemed like you wanted to be friends, at the grocery store."

"Your foot!" She leans over to look but bonks her head on the table. "Ow. Ow."

"Sit up." I take her wrist gently, and pull. There's a waft of baby-powder smell. No lilacs.

She jerks it back. "Respectful space in every place." But then her face looks sorry. Or confused, maybe.

I could just be imagining what I want to see.

"Just trying to help," I say.

"That was rude. I was rude, I mean. You barely know me."

"It's okay." This morning, I gave myself a talk. She doesn't re-member us. Not yet. Don't be surprised. Don't be hurt.

But it still burns to hear her say she barely knows me. "We could be friends," I say. Sounding a little too pathetic. I shut up and touch the paper in my pocket.

"Your other friends would miss you." Nia's eyes slide to another table. My old table, where all the superstars sit. Not my friends. Fol-lowers. Acolytes. The best listeners.

Including Mandi, today. Sherman is sitting next to her. He's shoveling food into his mouth, in slow motion. Mandi puts her fin-gertips on his chin and pushes up so his mouth closes.

"One should strive to be friends with everyone." I turn away and focus on Nia.

She's got the look down: zero makeup, unless you count the pale pink lips. Loose cardigan, grandma pants.

But something's wrong with her face. Her right cheek and eye are twitching. Cheek twitches. Then eye. Then cheek.

Nia tilts her head to the side and shakes it, like there's water in her ear.

"Are you feeling okay?" I ask.

"It's so cold in here." She grabs the front edges of her cardigan and pulls them around her.

Then she tosses her head, as if it's hair hanging loose and wild in her face.

As if part of her remembers how to be herself.

Someone slaps a tray down on the table. It's chess boy. He's easier to remember, now, seeing as how he finds me in the hallway every day.

"We're kind of having a private conversation," I tell him.

"No, we're not. It's fine." Nia pats the seat next to hers. Then she leans to whisper to me. "One should strive to be friends with everyone."

He sits down fast. "I heard that. And she's right."

"Seriously. Would you mind going somewhere else?" I ask. A thousand times nicer than what I really want to say.

He shakes his head. "Can't. I told them we'd eat with you today."

"Who?"

"The chess club."

"I don't play chess. Should I go?" Nia wraps her fingers around the edge of her tray.

"No. Don't. I mean, not without me."

"You can't leave," the boy says. "I promised them. I could lose my presidency." He's so upset he's talking with food in his mouth. I point. He clamps his lips shut.

Have to be nice. Can't spook Nia. Can't blow my cover.

"If you disappear now, I'll come to your next meeting," I tell him.

He raises one eyebrow. "Next three meetings."

"Fine. Just—go, okay?"

He retreats to the next table. Close enough to listen.

I feel claustrophobic, like the most popular monkey at the zoo. Everyone's watching me eat. They'd follow me to the toilet if they could. "Let's go outside," I say. To Founder's Park, that magical place where they all leave me alone.

"I shouldn't—I was going to study—there's a math quiz—" Her mouth makes excuses, but she's standing up anyway. Still holding her tray.

Some part of her wants to be with me.

"Ditch the tray," I tell her. "Right there on the table."

She obeys. But she can't stop looking back.

"Someone else will clean it up. They always do," I tell her. Wanting her to let it go. Just be a tiny bit bad.

Show me more real Nia.

"Oscar Banks is a superior person. I guess if you do it, then it's okay," she says. Quiet and confused.

Chess boy will probably take care of it. Maybe have my fork bronzed.

She follows me across the street to the park. We walk over the grass to the big tree. The place where we sat and she drew me.

It's not as hot today. The sky is bright blue, without any clouds. The only sound is a plane droning high up in the sky. And the squeak of kids' highlighters as they study.

"Let's sit," I say.

Nia frowns at the grass. "I just washed these pants."

I swallow a wave of disappointment. Pull a folder out of my backpack. *Paleomagnetism*, the label reads. I think I was supposed to study this stuff last night for a test. But I lost track of time at the shed.

When I drop the folder on the grass, she sits.

I nestle my crazy risk-taking butt in the grass. Unlace one of my shoes.

"What are you doing?" she asks.

"The grass feels good between your toes. Someone told me that once."

Blank stare tinged with fear. Fear of the crazy boy she so trustingly followed out to the park.

"Never mind." I tie the shoe back up.

"Birds bite." She tilts her head back and scans the sky. "Biting. Biting."

She's crazy, just like Sherman. Ruined.

No. I'm going to change that.

"The birds here are safe," I tell her. "All their teeth have been removed."

"Really?" Her smile is still so beautiful, if you don't look closely at her eyes.

"Nothing can hurt you in Candor." Except my father.

And me. Me, who lied to her. Should have warned her sooner. If I'd been honest, maybe we would have broken up. Maybe she would have made me help her leave.

But she'd still be safe.

She'd still be special.

I was wrong to be afraid of all the other possibilities.

"I have a present for you." I pull out the folded paper in my pocket and hand it to her. "Open it when you're alone."

Her mouth drops open, slack. She cradles the paper in both hands.

"Why?" A sharp word again. I savor it. But I don't answer.

The warning bell rings. All around us, kids cram their books into backpacks. Five minutes to class. My feet want to go, too.

The great are never late.

It's easy to push that one back, with Nia in front of me. She always made it easy to ignore what I'm supposed to do.

Nia hasn't moved. She's staring at her cupped hands. "A present from Oscar," she breathes. "A present for me."

"It's nothing."

"Oscar Banks is a superior person," she says. "He is a shining example."

"Don't believe everything you hear."

She picks it up in one hand. Starts unfolding with the other.

"For later. Not now," I warn her.

But she ignores me. Guess if my orders aren't buried in classical music, she doesn't feel obliged to listen.

Just one second of looking and she crumples it in a ball. "Art is a disease! Art is filthy!" she says in a low, shocked voice.

Then she throws it into the bushes. And instantly jumps to her feet to go get it. Must not litter.

It's the drawing she taped to my window—the one I hung in our museum. I hoped it would make her remember. Make her want to fight. But I haven't seen someone hate art so much since Mom started to change. It only took a few days before she realized what Dad was doing to her. Stealing my brother's memory, and her heart.

Then she was gone.

"No littering. I hate art. No littering," Nia mutters.

Not exactly the reaction I was hoping for.

"I hoped you'd like it," I tell her. "Maybe if you keep looking at it, you'll like it."

She gives one tiny shake of her head.

I had hoped for more. Something dramatic. But now I see that was stupid. What did I think was going to happen? She'd look at it and be cured? Muss up her hair, cut class, and take me to the woods?

She's got the crumpled ball in her hand. Tosses it from one hand to the other, like it's hot. "Why did you do that?"

"I want to be happy. I mean . . . I want you to be happy."

Cheek twitch. Eye twitch. Cheek twitch. "You're bad." Her voice is shaky. "Bad like birds. Birds with teeth."

You used to like that, I want to tell her. You even liked my teeth on your skin, sometimes.

"Don't get near me," she says. "I can't—don't—want to talk to you again."

"That's not very nice." But it makes me happy, in a sick way. She's being rude. And that's nothing like a good Candor girl.

"I don't think you deserve nice."

Nia doesn't say good-bye. Just walks away, slow, but every step firm. She knows where she's supposed to be.

She slams the paper into the first trash can she passes.

I should start forgetting. I should get back to my normal life. The one where I was in control of everything. Where I was safe.

But I can't take my eyes off her as she stumbles away. Broken, brainwashed Nia.

I love her. Still, even like this.

chapter 24

I WANT TO make it happen again.

Nia stopped being perfect, for a few seconds. If I could make it happen more—string those seconds closer, make them longer—I feel like I could get my girl back.

And I *will* make that happen.

I go to the shed. Pry open the wall behind the double stainless-steel sink. The bag is nearly full. I don't sneak even one into my mouth.

They're all for Nia now.

The walk home is quiet. I stare up at the stars. They're farther away than the ones on my ceiling. But they're more beautiful, because they're where they belong.

Maybe I should have made Nia go, early on. Helped her get where she would shine. But I was selfish. It makes me mad. At me. At my father. At the Messages.

I walk past a squat green speaker, half-hidden in the bushes. It's not on at night. But I still hate it. I give it a hard kick.

It doesn't move. But my toes throb. A sliver of pain reminds me of the bandage I'm still wearing on my foot.

I'm nearly home when I hear the squeak of a sneaker behind me.

"There's a curfew." The voice is familiar, but wrong somehow. Changed.

I shove the bag deeper in my pants pocket and turn around.

He shines a light straight in my eyes. "TAG patrol."

"Drop it," I tell Sherman.

But he keeps it steady. I bat at the light. It swings away. There's a cracking noise when it hits the sidewalk.

"Gosh darn it all!" Sherman drops to his knees to grab the light. But my foot gets to it first.

Plunk. Into the storm sewer.

"Better run home and get another one," I say.

Sherman stands and smoothes the front of his sweatshirt. It has three letters across the chest: TAG. "Why'd you do that?" he asks. "I said I was on patrol."

"Why, exactly? To blind people with flashlights?"

"Teens Against Graffiti keeps your streets beautiful. Anyone can join us." He says it so smoothly, I wonder if Dad has made a Message to help Mandi's pet project. "I'm sorry about the light. We should never harm others."

What a good boy, spouting Messages. He's doing better than when I saw him in the ER. No shakes. No crazy talk. He's a fully functioning product of Candor.

His face has changed the most. The squinty weasel look and smirk are missing. They ironed him out into a smooth Candor boy.

Is his brain missing all the wrinkles, too? Does he remember anything?

Sherman mutters something. His arms flap at his sides like he's a penguin roaming the streets in Candor. I was wrong. He's still living in crazy town.

"Are you okay?" I ask. The Messages want me to care. But I don't, not really. Not much.

"Have you seen my secrets?" he asks.

"Uh—no." Let's hope they stay gone, too.

"Slippery shiny silver secrets." Sherman holds both hands up, with his fingers in a round shape. Like a CD. "I only need one. It's special. I just don't . . . remember. . . ."

Even the Listening Room didn't make me safe. I should have personally shoved the kid in the back of Frank's truck. Made sure he was gone forever.

"I have to go," I tell him. Before seeing me shakes something else loose in his brain.

"No! State—" Sherman clears his throat. "State your business. Or I'll call you in."

My fists clench like they've got their own memories. I came so close to beating him into the squishy Florida sod that night.

It would still feel good.

A walkie-talkie crackles on his waist. He grabs it and meets my eyes for the first time. "Patrol three, POI," he says into the radio. "Hostile."

Maybe I should be scared. But it's Mandi's little club. How dangerous could they be? Will they petition me to death?

But they could tell on me. No need for Dad to know I was out tonight. So maybe I need to stick around until I come up with a good excuse.

Then I'll be free.

A girl's voice answers. "Maintain position. I'm two blocks away."

Not just any girl. Mandi. All my special friends are out tonight.

"Bringing in the big boss, huh?" I ask.

When Mandi rounds the corner, his head swivels to watch. Her pink sweatshirt has sparkles that catch the streetlights. Either her jogging shoes are brand-new or she spent an hour scrubbing away every mark.

I slide my hand in my pocket. Make sure my secret is still safe. Yes. My fingers slide over the little bumps, feel the pieces move in the bag.

"There's a curfew," Mandi says. Her eyes flick over me.

"So why aren't you home?" I ask her. "Surely there's some kind of quiz tomorrow."

"Our community is in jeopardy," she says. "Besides, I did my homework in study hall."

"What a relief. Yale almost slipped between your fingers."

"Yale likes a well-rounded student." Her smile is smug.

"They big on running fake police patrols these days?"

Sherman fumbles with his sweatshirt pocket. "We're not the police. We're TAG."

"You mentioned that," I tell him.

He's still trying to yank something out. A rabbit? A gun? I can't help laughing.

"For gosh sake," Mandi snaps. Then she reaches into his pocket and pulls out a gold badge. Dangles it in front of his nose.

Sherman looks surprised. "Always be courteous," he reminds her.

Mandi rolls her eyes and sucks in a deep breath. "You're right. I'm sorry."

He takes it and licks his lips. Lifts his chin so our eyes meet and holds the badge high. But it shakes in his hand. The boy's scared of me.

"TAG patrol," he says loudly.

A dog barks in the house behind us. Sherman jumps and the badge flops to the sidewalk.

Mandi picks it up and puts it in her pocket.

"He seems a little off," I tell Mandi.

"Yeah." She looks at Sherman. "Ever since he . . . went away—things have been different."

"You love him?" The question pops out of my mouth like it's a Message that's been waiting for the perfect moment. I didn't even know it was in me.

Her face softens into a smile. She looks at him like he's sculpted from gold. "Sherman Golub is my destiny."

"I don't know why you like me," Sherman says. He's smiling back, all melty. "I'm the luckiest guy in the world."

The Listening Room gave him what he wanted. Sherman has no idea why Mandi wants him. But he knows it can't be for real, still. I feel a little sorry for him.

Mandi's radio beeps. Snookums staring time is over. She steps away to talk into the radio. The only person left for Sherman to stare at is me.

And he looks a little too hard. "What's that?" Sherman points at my pocket.

At the corner of the brown bag sticking out. Leave it to Sherman to sniff out food.

"Nothing." I jam it back in.

But sweet little Mandi drops her radio and shoves her hand in my pocket.

I yank her arm away. But she's got the bag. It slips out of her hand and smacks onto the sidewalk. The rubber band holding it closed snaps.

All my precious M&M's go rolling for the sewer.

"No!" I'm on my knees, saving them, all of them, for her.

But Mandi is there, too. Pushing them away. Shoving them into the drain. They rain into the water below. The sound is too loud for such tiny little things.

"Chocolate is bad for you," she says. Firm, like she's my mother. "It makes you fat, and it gives you zits, and it's not nutritious."

Combine a former beauty queen with the Messages and you have an anti-chocolate crusader. I'm surprised there hasn't been a petition.

"I need them." I scrabble away from her on the sidewalk, but she pushes forward on her hands and knees. Like a tiger hunting.

She slaps at my hand and it opens. Traitor. All of them gone, in the grass.

Sherman joins on the fun, stomping on them. Smashing my hope into multicolored bits on the grass.

"Bad treats! No good!" he says.

My face feels wet. Cold. Tears? Who put them there? Who let them come out, now?

I never cry.

Mandi's voice is gentle. "It's for the best."

"You don't know how much I needed those," I tell her.

We're sitting on the grass. Me flat on my wimp ass, breathing like I ran a race. Her on her knees. This time I'm the one who's beat.

She leans forward and places one cold hand on my cheek. "Addiction is an ugly thing," she whispers.

Our eyes meet and something tugs at me. I want to tell her.

You don't even know you're hooked, Mandi Able.

But her radio squawks again, something about litter in sector two. "Go home," she says.

My fingers find one lump in the grass. Two.

A little dirty, maybe. But I can brush them off.

"I'm going." I wrap my fingers around the candy that melts in your mouth, not in your hands.

Safe.

"We won't tell," she says.

I forgot to be afraid of that. As soon as I saw the candy rolling away, I knew what I was really afraid of. Losing my shot at making Nia remember.

"But you always tell," I say.

"Let's call it a favor." Mandi looks at Sherman. "You can pay us back later."

"Secrets!" Sherman shouts.

Mandi and I shush him at the same time.

"Yes," she says, her voice low. "Oscar will help us with the secrets."

That sounds like a bad idea. But she's giving me an out and I need to take it.

"Thanks," I tell Mandi. "I'll go home now."

I walk that way. They go the other way, together.

I keep my fist tight around the two M&M's I have left. All the way home.

chapter 25

I FOLLOW NIA after school. She's not riding her board anymore. Now she has a shiny pink NEV with white pinstripes and a license plate that reads SWEET.

She said she doesn't want to talk to me. That will make things harder. But I'll find a way. Today.

She's alone. No friends to drop off. Just her, and me, going somewhere. Hopefully somewhere alone.

Nia swings into a place right behind the post office. Then she's out, holding a brown-wrapped package. Moving fast.

Maybe nobody else will be near her. I have to try.

I block in two big SUVs and follow. But not too close.

The post office is a tall cylinder, painted blue with white metal awnings jutting over the doors and windows. Some famous architect designed it. Dad brags about it in all the brochures. Everything comes here: mail and boxes. No risky outsiders coming by our houses every day. No ugly mailboxes, either.

People think they love picking up their mail. They say it's old-fashioned community building.

I say Dad thinks of everything. Almost.

Nia heaves open one of the heavy doors and bounces inside.

I check my pocket to make sure I still have what I need.

It's just Nia and me in the little lobby. The doors to the inside part are shut tight. This is my chance.

"I miss you," I say.

Not what I planned. Not even on the top fifty opening lines. More like the bottom three.

"Oscar?" Her hand shoots into her bag. I hear the crackle of paper. "I don't want . . ."

Can't scare her. I rewind into normal. "Do you have change for a stamp?" I ask.

It actually works. Candor kids can't not be helpful. She sets down her box and rummages through the monogrammed tote. Pink letters and ribbons ring the edge.

Can't waste time. Someone could walk in any second.

Closer. Closer. Soon I'm just a foot away. "Want to try something?" I ask.

Great. First I sound pathetic. Now I sound like a pervy old man.

"No more presents, please. Even if—" Her eyes move over my face. "Even if you're Oscar Banks."

She holds the change out. I open my hand to accept it. The coins feel warm, as if they've been riding along in her pocket. I close my fingers around them slowly.

Our eyes meet. Something shifts in her face. The sweetness drops for a second. She remembers something, I can tell.

"Close your eyes," I whisper.

She obeys. Then her eyes pop open. "You do bad things."

What does she remember? Is this about the art I gave her at lunch? Or does she know something about our past? "Oscar Banks is a superior person," I remind her.

She nods slowly. Closes her eyes again.

I yank the bag out of my pocket and rip it open. A precious M&M is between my thumb and finger. It's red.

I look outside. Nobody's near the post office.

Then I put my other thumb on her chin and tug gently. Her bottom lip drops down. Pink tongue, poking out. Just a tiny bit.

I drag in a deep breath and lean close. My hand relaxes and the candy pings onto the floor.

Nia's eyes fly open. She slaps both hands over her mouth. "What are you doing?"

"One more second," I plead.

"I have to send this package. I have to get the mail. I have to get home and do homework. Academics are our top priority."

The outer door to the lobby flies open. A man in a suit and tie walks in. Doesn't bother to look at us. Goes straight inside.

His shoe barely misses the candy on the floor.

We're safe. But my heart is pounding like I've been caught.

Nia picks up her box. "I have to go."

"Wait. It's for school. If you don't help me, I'll flunk the lab. Please." I don't care how desperate I sound. I'm so close. I don't want to wait. "Academics are our top priority, like you said."

"What class is this for?" she asks.

"Bio. Don't worry. Would I hurt you?" I give her the patented Oscar smile that never used to work on her. The one all the other girls like.

She sighs and squeezes her eyes shut. Opens her mouth wide. Obedient baby bird. The old Nia never would have done that. But for now, her obedience is handy.

I pick up the chocolate. Wipe it on my pants. Drop it on her tongue.

"Chew."

She does. Her eyes pop open, wide. "Chocolate."

"M&M's." I wait for something to show on her face. More memories. Happiness. But she just looks disgusted.

"This isn't healthy." She sticks out her tongue. It has tiny red candy bits on it.

"Don't you like it?"

Nia reaches into her tote bag and pulls out a thick pack of Kleenex. She picks one and wipes her tongue.

"It won't kill you," I say.

She balls the Kleenex into her fist. "Not even vanilla frozen yogurt tastes that good."

I feel the plastic bag in my pocket. There's one left. "Want to try again?"

The inside door opens. Suit man is leaving. Still moving fast. He leaves without looking. I think. I hope.

It breaks the spell.

"I don't want any." Nia hoists her tote bag higher on her shoulder, like she's ready to go. Her hand runs up and down the slippery ribbon strap. "I had a dream about you."

That has to be good. Stay cool. Casual. "Oh, yeah?" I feel sweat forming on the back of my neck. "Tell me."

Nia looks up at the ceiling. "It was after you gave me that horrible art. I dreamed about pieces of paper, hundreds of them. They were clipped to clotheslines. And you were there, looking at them."

"What was on the paper?"

Her hand grips the strap so tight that her knuckles turn white. "The papers were so pretty. And we were laughing, and—"

The stupid pushy dork inside me speaks up. "We kissed, didn't we?"

She jumps like she's been shocked. "Personal space in every place!"

"It was just a dream." I say it to make her feel better. But it's a lie.

That dream wasn't random. Part of her remembers.

I just have to keep trying.

"Package. Have to send my package," Nia mutters. She picks up the brown box and goes to push open the door to the inside part of the post office.

I've been lucky. I won't push more. Not today. "See you."

But then she looks back at me. Her eyes are sharp now. "What kind of experiment was that?"

I stare, stupid with happiness. Too slow. Not remembering the lie I told her two minutes ago.

"With the candy?" A wicked look flits across her face, just a second. Like a butterfly flying over a snow bank. It doesn't belong. But it's beautiful.

"Oh. It was—a memory thing. To see if tastes make you remember things. But don't tell. It's for the science fair."

She nods wisely. "Sorry it didn't work."

"Maybe you need more." I hold up the plastic bag. One lonely green M&M.

Nia shakes her head. "Candy is unhealthy."

"It's a tiny little bit." I take the bag and stuff it in between her textbooks. "For later."

"I'll just throw that away," she warns.

"Do what you want."

"I have to go." Nia pushes open the door, then looks back at me. "Bye, Candy Man."

"You used to call me Picasso," I say. But the door's already slammed shut.

chapter 26

NIA STAYS AWAY after the post office. Skitters away if we pass in the hall. Sits at a table full of kids, staring at a book.

I can never catch her eye. I can't tell if something different is unfolding inside. She remembered something in the post office. Did it stick around? Is that why she doesn't want to talk to me?

But I don't chase her. Pushing her might make the real Nia hide. Or disappear. I want her to remember. And then I want her to come to me.

I avoid Mandi. As much as I want Nia to remember, I want Mandi to forget that night. How I was out after curfew, with something forbidden.

And no good excuse.

There are plenty of cardigan-wearing girls to sit with. I can't escape. One goes away and another one shows up. They all audition to be my next girlfriend. I nod and smile. It's the safe thing to do. Someone might be watching. But I never hear a word they say.

If I was the kind of person who needed company, I'd be lonely.

After my third girlfriend candidate of the day tries to trap me in an after-school SAT review, I decide to hide.

So I go to Mandi's and my special place: the movie theater.

They always let us in for free. Being Campbell's kid pays all kinds of dividends. Mandi used to bring her book light and a bag of baby carrots. I scored cartons of milk from the concession stand.

Nobody ever bothered us there. No begging for help with math homework. Or asking Mandi if she'd run a bake sale to save the cockroaches of Antarctica.

We didn't talk. Did regular homework first. Then extra credit. It all got done faster if we sat together. We were always trying to prove who was smarter. Faster. Better.

Maybe it was weird. But it was our thing. I liked being somewhere dark, where people might not notice me. I got to be a normal kid sitting in the theater conjugating French verbs.

Sometimes I miss it. Not that I'd trade Nia—if I still had her. But Mandi was okay when she wasn't wound up.

Today I bring my calc book and a bag of celery sticks. It's stadium-style seating, so I go to the bottom of the balcony, where the rail blocks half the screen and you can prop your feet up. It was our spot.

Now it's all for me.

I put in my earplugs when the previews start. The dark theater feels like sliding under a warm blanket in winter. Cozy and alone.

When Mandi sits in the chair next to me, I'm confused for a split second. Are we still dating? Was it all a dream? Where are her books?

She yanks the earplugs from my ears. I try to grab them back, but she's too quick.

"Payback time," she says. "I mean—can we talk? I'm hoping you can do me a favor."

"I paid you back for the frozen yogurt months ago," I say. Even though I know what she means.

Somebody shushes us from the back. Mandi swings her head to give them an evil look. It might be dark, but I'll bet they feel the crazy glare coming from her eyes. I guess that part of her body doesn't have to listen to the Messages.

"Always be courteous," I mutter. Just to tweak her a little, like old times.

"I know that." Mandi turns back around. "I need you to help him."

"You mean Sherman."

She looks around. So do I. Just one person—the shusher—sitting in the back. Her head swings back to me. "He's fine for hours. But then he starts talking about needing his secrets."

"Sounds crazy to me."

"He drools and flaps his arms and sometimes . . . sometimes he even tries to hurt himself." Mandi looks down in her lap.

I look, too—expecting to see a book or something else productive. But there are just her hands. Squeezed together tight.

"Sherman Golub is my destiny," she whispers.

"I can't say I agree," I tell her.

"You don't understand. I would do anything to help him."

She looks so sad and worried. I almost put my hand on top of hers. Then I remember where we are. Who we are.

"He says you have the secret he needs," she says.

"I have no idea what he's talking about."

She lets out a huff of air and settles back into her seat. We both stare at the screen. There's a dog running around someone's backyard with a hose in its mouth. Giggling sister and brother chase it. All good clean Candor movie fun.

"You owe me," she says. "I could have told about the curfew."

"I know." But it's not enough. Sherman messes everything up. If I give him more Messages, he'll just make things worse.

Her head swivels and she narrows her eyes at me. "I might still do it. I could tell your father about *everything*."

My body freezes. I can only breathe. And blink. Stare at the dog on the screen running through a field. Happy dog. Scared Oscar. Mean Mandi.

What did Sherman tell her? They were together before the Listening Room. There was time for him to spill the beans, just like he did with Nia.

He's like a stain that just keeps spreading.

"Now you're listening," she says.

I search my memory for a Message to remind her of: something to make her back off. Something about loyalty or friendship or . . . But I can't think of anything.

If she tells, I'm sunk. My father will believe anything she says. She's one of his masterpieces.

"Your father thinks you're perfect. But he's wrong," she says.

My lips form the words but I can't get sound to come out. *You're wrong. You're crazy. You don't know what you're talking about.*

But she does, at least a little.

"You have to do what I say," she says.

I finally force my lips open. "I'll tell him you're lying."

"I have proof."

"What kind . . . where did you . . . ?" What did Sherman tell her?

"You dropped them in the grass. Duh."

Candy. She's still talking about candy. As if that's the big Oscar shocker. Relief reminds me: I'm in charge. How did I forget?

I grab both her wrists and pull so we're facing each other. "If you tell, I'll get even. I promise."

She lets out a shocked gasp and yanks her hands free. "Respectful space in every place, mister."

"Sorry." I mutter.

Why shouldn't I tell my father something tonight, something that will send her straight to the Listening Room? I already got Sherman put there. It would be best, maybe, if she went, too.

But I don't know if I can do it again. I watched Nia disappear. Saw Sherman sick, in the emergency room. Mandi was my girlfriend for two years. Don't I owe her something for putting up with me?

Don't I owe Sherman something? A small something? Pain relief, maybe. Nothing more.

"I don't do anything for free," I tell her.

"I'll pay."

"I don't need money."

"What do you want?" she asks.

I know what I wanted from her a few months ago. But now? I'm not sure.

"There's nothing," I tell her.

"You need my help with Nia," she says.

She must be able to see my surprised face in the dark, because she laughs. "I see you chasing her. But she's hiding from you."

I hate that anyone's seen it. It means I've been sloppy. Out of control.

Maybe I do need her help. "What would you do?" I ask.

"Girls listen to other girls, Oscar. I could tell her how nice you are. What a good boyfriend you are."

We both snort at the same time. Which turns into laughing. The guy in the back shushes us.

Mandi stops laughing. "Do we have a deal?"

I'd do anything for Nia. Even this.

"It's a deal," I tell her.

She holds her hand out. I take it and shake it. I forgot how small her fingers are, how cold they feel.

"So where are they?" she asks.

"You deliver Nia. I'll deliver the secret." A few of them: ones that will make my life easier. Like giving me a loyal assistant. And making sure Sherman's lips stay shut.

"Fine. I'll go first." Mandi stands up. Her chair flops shut. "Then it's your turn. I'll be waiting."

And I'll be paranoid. Waiting every day for her to tell about the candy. Or maybe more. I still wonder what she knows. I always will. She could hand my brain to Dad on a silver platter.

Or maybe she'll help me. Convince Nia I'm a good guy. Give me the openings I need to keep digging for the real girl.

It's worth the risk.

Besides, I'm not sure I have any other choice.

chapter 27

MANDI DELIVERS A few days later.

"Come to the crayon swap," she tells me in the long lunch line for skim milk. "Nia will be there. And she'll be looking for you."

"I don't think she'd turn her art stuff in." Even if her brain is pickled.

She shakes her head. Her smile is triumphant. "She'll be working the table. Don't forget, you owe *me* after that."

I remember when Nia crumpled up the TAG poster. Now she's one of them.

"*If* she's really there. And *if* she talks with me."

Mandi rolls her eyes and lowers her voice. "Of course she'll be there. Nia's one of my best TAGers."

When we lived in Chicago, they had a gun-swap program. People brought in guns and got sneakers instead. It didn't seem to stop people from shooting each other. But at least they had nice shoes.

These days, there are things as dangerous as guns in Candor, if you ask TAG.

Markers. Glitter glue. Pipe cleaners.

There are posters all over town:

CRAYONS FOR CALCULATORS
Bring your art supplies and further your future!

TAG sponsors it.

My next big chance.

Nia has nearly vanished. It's like she has a new superpower: she can disappear whenever I get within twenty feet. I guess she's done believing I'm a superior person.

And now she's joined TAG. I see her at their petition tables. Selling cupcakes. Avoiding me, like always.

I've tried reminding her eyes with what she used to be, with the art she drew. Then I tried reminding her mouth with the candy. The crayon swap gives me a new idea.

Scent.

I drop a flamingo postcard to one of my former clients. Clint. He helps me get whatever I need. Nobody's more creative with their shipping and packaging.

ONE BOX OF SCENTED MARKERS.
INCLUDE PURPLE ONE. MUST SMELL LIKE LILACS.

He'll obey, because he knows he should. Not because my Messages tell him to. I give my people on the outside free will.

The paycheck makes their decisions for them now.

The line is twenty-three people long when I get to the swap in front of the ice-cream parlor. It's hot outside and the sun is still strong. But the kids stand precisely, one behind the other, exactly in the middle of the sidewalk. They're holding paper bags jammed with construction paper and half-used crayons. Nobody fans themselves or complains about the heat.

Everyone looks like they're in line to see Santa Claus. You'd think they'd look sad. Or mad. Or something besides overjoyed.

I tap the shoulder of the kid in front of me. He's seven, maybe eight. His supplies are in a red bucket on the sidewalk.

"Why are you here?" I ask him.

His smile stretches his cheeks tight. He bounces a little on his sneaker toes. "Art is boring," he says. "I don't need this stuff."

I keep my voice low. "I'll bet you used to like it."

He shrugs. "Not anymore. I want a calculator. A silver one."

"It's your lucky day."

"It sure is, mister!"

The line inches ahead and he kicks his bucket forward. Pulls his foot away fast, like it might get burned.

This is Dad's dream come true. He always said art was useless. The Messages agreed, of course. But it never went this far.

Nia's graffiti gave him the opening he wanted. I'm sure he's feeding Messages to all of us saying TAG is right: crayons bad, calculators good.

Nia is at the table. She takes buckets of supplies and dumps them in big black plastic trash bags. It's sick. This is all about erasing the thing she loves—or loved. Now she's handing over calculators with a sweet smile.

I grip the box of markers tight in my hand. I once read that smells bring back memories better than any other of the senses. This has to work.

Mandi's working the line. Thanking people for coming. Handing the excited little rascals bottles of water so they don't drop before they hand over the goods.

When Mandi gets to me, I give her my best fake smile. "What a great idea. Get rid of those crayons before something bad happens."

She looks pleased. "Everybody says it's the best TAG initiative yet."

I lower my voice and look around before I continue. "I mean, imagine . . . some stupid kid might actually have made *art*."

Mandi gets quieter, too. "Don't forget," she says. "You owe me."

"I've got what you want."

"Here?" She presses her lips together and her eyes get big.

"Elsewhere."

I made the CD last night. It's mostly flutes and only a few Messages. They aim to make Sherman less crazy. And also to forget all my secrets. But I couldn't resist just one fun one: *You are worthy.* It's sad he knows Mandi can't really want him. My parting gift.

"I'll hide them under your porch swing tonight," I tell her. "Get them before the morning."

Her smile comes back, even brighter than before. "Thank you for coming." Her voice is loud and happy again.

The line moves. I go forward. She walks back. I can focus on Nia again. Nia, with her curls brushed into a high, bouncy ponytail. Pink nails. Pink lips.

When I get to the front, I set the markers on the table in front of her. All except the purple one. I keep that in my hand.

She doesn't look up at first. Too busy writing important notes about the bucket of crayons she just trashed.

I wait.

Then Nia looks up. Her head jerks back a little, surprised. "It's you! Mandi said you'd come."

A big smile settles on my face. She's talking to me. And she's beautiful, even if she almost looks like all the others. "You're not going to run away, are you?"

"No, I'm working. And Mandi said—never mind." Her cheeks flush red. I've never seen her blush before. "Do you have crayons?" she asks.

Looks like Mandi has done her job. Now it's my turn. I push the box of markers closer. "For you."

Her eyes stay on me. She licks her lips. Remembering M&M's? Or another time? Then she takes in a deep breath and tips the markers out onto the table. Her long fingers nudge them across the table as she counts them.

Then I uncap the purple one. "Forgot this one."

It's easy to wave it under her nose. She's busy being busy.

She does exactly what I want her to do. Closes her eyes and moves her face closer to the marker. "It's lilac," she says.

The smell that used to whisper from her skin. I'll never forget it. How could she?

"Do you remember?" I ask.

Nia's eyes snap open. She shovels my markers into the trash bag without looking at me.

"Keep the purple one," I tell her.

But she makes a big show of capping it and tossing it into the bag. "Art is a disease," she mutters.

"That's what all the kids are saying these days." I mean it to sound like a joke, but it comes out serious.

Nia slaps a silver calculator in front of me. "Thank you for coming." Her voice is flat.

I bend over the table so she's forced to look at me. "If it makes you remember, I'll be waiting at our place. Every night."

"Stop bugging me." Her voice is low but intense.

"Then start remembering."

She gestures to the kid behind me. I step away. For now I'll give her more space. More time.

And pray she decides she doesn't need it anymore.

Maybe as soon as tonight.

chapter 28

I WAIT AT the shed, five nights in a row. Jittery. Sure she won't come. But hoping anyway.

She doesn't.

When I get home, I stare at my books and pretend nothing is wrong. But all I can do is ask the same questions every night: Why doesn't she come to the shed? Is it the TAG patrols? Her parents? Maybe she can't sneak out. I should have picked an easier way to meet.

Or she still doesn't remember.

One night I fall asleep at my desk. I wake up when Dad opens my door.

It's not even light out yet.

"Come with me," he says. "She needs you."

I stare at him. *Pretend everything's normal,* I remind myself. *Don't give anything up.* "Who?" I ask.

"Your little friend is sick. She's asking for you." He turns and I hear him *thump-thump*ing down the steps.

Nia remembers. She must be asking for me.

But she's sick. And Dad's seen her—knows where she is, too. That means she must have done something stupid again.

I look around my room, as if there's something I can grab, some magic powder or elixir that will save her. But all I've got is my Yale calendar and a stack of textbooks.

"Hurry up!" Dad yells.

Maybe it's the flu. Or she broke her leg. That would be good news, in a sad way.

He drives. I ask questions he mostly ignores.

"What's wrong with her?"

He shakes his head like it's impossible to explain.

"Does she have the flu? Did she break something?"

This time he just squints ahead. Grips the wheel, like he's driving us through a snowstorm.

"Will she be okay?" My voice cracks.

Dad glances at me. "She's in the best care. We won't let her stay sick."

That makes me shiver. Maybe I don't want to hear more.

We pass Nia's street, but we don't stop. Straight through downtown, too, past the Listening Room. There's only one place left. A bad news place. I force the words through gritted teeth. "Where are we going?"

"Hospital."

Fear rockets through my body. I remember Sherman stumbling into the ER. Drooling, talking crazy. Is that what's happened to her? I want to ask more questions. But I'm afraid it will make him change his mind. He won't let me see her.

And I have to see her. Even if there's nothing left.

Dad's muttering to himself under his breath now, like a crazy man. He does that when he's stressed. Like he's talking himself into something, or out of something. An entire whispered conversation.

I hear bits of what he's saying.

"Fool girl. Everything going for her."

We pull into the hospital parking lot and he presses his lips together. They're sealed so tight, the skin is white around them.

"Why would she ever want to leave?" he asks.

"Leave? Like, run away?" My greatest fear before they changed her. And she tries it now?

"We don't say 'run away.' Especially in front of her folks. They're taking it hard." Dad sets toward the doors in a fast walk. I have to break into a half-jog to keep up.

This is the worse thing she could have done.

Running away, leaving, taking a long walk in the woods: whatever you call it, they're all suicide in Candor without my help. Once you leave the reach of the speakers, you can't hear the Messages. We're all hooked. Some people only need a few quiet hours before the withdrawal sets in. That's why my clients get an MP3 player and an extra set of batteries.

Without it, they'll go crazy.

We hurry past the welcome desk, the gift shop, the fountain with pennies covering the bottom. The water is too loud. *This is serious*, I want to shout. *Stop making noise.*

Dad opens a janitor's closet and motions for me to follow him.

"We need brooms?" I ask. Not trying to be funny. Just not understanding.

He sighs and yanks on my elbow. I stumble in and he shuts the door.

Dad pushes open a door on the other side of the closet. Hurries ahead.

I follow him down a short, wide hallway to a round nurse's station. Four doors sit in the wall behind the station. They're all closed. No windows.

The man behind the desk doesn't even look up. Dad steps to the second door from the left. He walks in, but I stay behind.

Seeing her changed is torture. But seeing her sick—crazy sick—will be worse. Especially since it's my fault, at least partly. I don't know if I can handle it.

I close my eyes and picture her. That night I saw her on the skateboard. When we kissed in the pool. Her face when she saw the museum I made for her. If I can remember, she's not gone.

Then I walk into the room.

There's music playing, piano and flutes. I see two people sitting in chairs—my dad and someone, someone that doesn't matter, someone not worth looking at. My eyes shoot to the hospital bed, but I don't know where to start looking.

Start at the bottom. Her feet are strapped down with thick black rubber over white sheets. My eyes travel up, slow, slow. Her wrists are strapped down, too. Hands bunched into fists. They're trembling. Now I see her whole body is trembling under that sheet.

All the pictures from the black folder fill my mind. I can't look.

"Say hello, Oscar," Dad barks.

"Oscar's here?" Her voice is high-pitched and crackly.

It startles me enough to do it. I look. Golden hair fanned over a pillow. Perky nose. Scratches down her cheeks. Lips split and bloody, with bits of pink lipstick around the edge.

Familiar, yes.

But not Nia.

Mandi's eyes open, slowly, slowly, like there are weights attached to her eyelids.

The relief makes me want to laugh. Grab my father and dance a jig around her hospital bed. Sorry to see you here, Mandi. But it doesn't matter, not as long as it's not Nia.

"I'm sorry you're sick," I say. Sounding too happy. Or hysterical.

Her lip lifts in a snarl. "I'll kill you," she growls. "You think you can beat me?"

Psychosis isn't just about hurting yourself. I take a step back.

Now I understand why Dad's confused. Why would Mandi run away? She's the Candor mold, the one they make all the other girls match.

"We found her in the woods," a woman's voice says. It's Mrs. Able, Mandi's mother. The woman who has made me a thousand oatmeal cookies and poured me a swimming pool's worth of milk to go with them.

"Where's Daddy?" Mandi giggles.

"Getting his tetanus shot, you little monster," her mother snaps. Then she lets out a gallon of tears.

"It's natural to be angry." Dad's voice is folksy, soothing, like he's seen this a hundred times. I guess he has. Is this what he does all those late nights and Sunday afternoons, when he has to "go to work"?

Of course it is. I always knew it. I just hadn't seen it before.

"Why was she in the woods?" I ask.

Mandi's mother stands up and steps closer to her daughter. Staring at her like she's a stranger. "Mandi had a suitcase with her. Sashes, her state crown, her baton . . . I thought we'd thrown it all away."

Mandi tries to sit up. "Only three weeks until states!" she shouts.

"You don't compete anymore, honey." Her mother reaches for her. But Mandi bares her even, white teeth. Mrs. Able jumps back.

"You said I couldn't win," Mandi growls. "You lied to me."

"Pageants are a waste of time, honey." Her mother gives Dad a nervous look. "Right? Don't you remember?"

"I am worthy. I am *worthy!*" Mandi shakes her head from side to side. "*WORTHY! WORTHY!*"

I am worthy. The little gift I put on Sherman's new CD. It was only for him. It was just supposed to make him happy.

But Mandi must have listened, too. That Message meant something very different to her. I wonder if her parents used boosters to counterprogram her, to make her hate pageants.

All it took was one Message to push her back to her old self. My Message.

My screwup.

"How did this happen?" Mandi's mother asks. She looks at me before she continues. The next words come slow, like she's choosing them carefully. "This isn't what we . . . expected."

Dad's answer makes me wonder if he forgot I'm in the room. "You're right. It's not what you paid for. And it's not what *we* delivered." Dad crouches by Mrs. Able and stares into her eyes. "Someone's . . . influenced your girl. Someone unauthorized."

"You'll fix her. You'll fix my Amanda." She swallows hard.

"I promise," he says. "And when I find the culprit, we'll fix him, too."

When he realizes what I'm hearing, what will he do? They're talking about the Messages. Doesn't he think I'll ask questions? Put things together?

Or maybe he's used to being safe, too.

"Oscar." Dad looks at me.

My heart beats so fast it hurts. "Yes?"

"Mandi's been asking for you, telling us strange things."

That's why he wanted me to come. This isn't a visit. It's an interrogation. I feel his eyes steady on me. Watching everything.

"Like what?" I ask, keeping my words slow and steady. Not like my heart. It's pounding.

Mandi barks out a loud laugh and licks her lips fast, over and over. "Silvery round secrets!"

"What's that mean?" Dad asks.

"I have no idea." Mandi's a new kind of threat now. Between her and Sherman, how will I fix things?

"Sherman shared his secrets." Mandi licks her lips. "Don't be mad, Oscar."

"What do you know?" Dad asks. Not *do you know anything?* or *can you help?* Those are his usual questions.

That tells me everything. It's not safe for me anymore. He's suspicious. He'll start looking for things. Watching everything. Did I hide it all well enough? What happens if he finds something, anything?

Keep it casual. Swallow my fear. "All I know is, she's been weird lately."

"Weird how?"

"Kind of mean, I guess. Grouchy."

Mandi is pulling her hands up, fighting the restraints. "Free Miss Charm Texas!" she shouts.

"You know nothing about these . . . secrets?" Dad asks. "Your name keeps coming up. So tell me the truth, son."

His commands used to work. But now it's like another Message. Washing over me. It doesn't last. Doesn't matter.

So I take a second to listen to the Messages. Find out what I'm supposed to believe. And I feed him a few Messages. "Never keep secrets from your parents," I say. "Trust your parents with everything."

Dad lets out a loud, long breath. His face relaxes. Almost looks proud.

"I wish I could help," I add.

"You can go," he says.

I look at Mandi. Her crazy bloodshot eyes stare back.

"Always share with your friends," she croaks.

I put my hand on the knob.

"I am worthy!" she yells.

Me and my guilty conscience walk out the door.

chapter 29

DAD LETS ME leave without him.

"I'll stay with Mandi's mother awhile," he says. Hands me his keys.

I don't ask how he'll get home. A guy like my dad can't walk five feet down the street without some good listener wanting to drive him somewhere.

"Better go make some rye toast," I say.

"Good man."

The suspicious look has left his eyes. Why? Because he suddenly trusts me again? Or because he already has a plan for watching me? Or changing me?

Mandi got him thinking. He'll watch me more now. All the time, maybe.

I have to see Nia before that happens. No more waiting for her to come to me.

So I go to her house. It's early, just past breakfast time. But I know all good Candor citizens have been up for at least an hour.

Her father answers. Tense smile. But he shakes my hand like we're two old farts meeting on the golf course. "Oscar Banks," he says. "Nia's out back, skimming the pool."

He leaves me alone to walk through the house to the back doors. It's that easy. All this time I was watching her, waiting for an opportunity. I could have just knocked on her door.

But she still might kick me out.

Nia's dad is washing dishes in the kitchen. *Go slow*, I remind myself. *Act like you don't care.* I force myself to look around. They bought a Rockdale model. One of Dad's most popular houses. He designed it for our old family: four beds, three baths, a study for him, and a sunroom for Mom's art.

Their furniture looks old—not antique, just worn out. Nia told me once that they only bought new stuff for the front porch, because that's where people would see it.

I get to the sliding doors and stop to look out.

Nia is skimming the pool and dumping out bugs in the bushes. Her head is covered in an old-lady flowered hat.

It's not a huge pool like ours. But it's deep, with no shallow end, like it was made just for jumping in.

I open the doors. Shut them. We're alone together.

I didn't plan any of this. There was no time to decide what to say. Now I don't know where to start. I need her. I want her. I'm sick of waiting.

But all those things will scare her.

"How are you?" I ask.

"Oscar! Why are you—what—I'm, um, wonderful," she says. Her voice is girly and high-pitched.

"Mandi is sick," I say. It's not why I'm here. But it pops out. I have to tell someone. "She tried to run away and now she's in the hospital."

Now Nia takes off her sunglasses. She furrows her brow. "That's so sad. Why would anyone want to leave Candor?"

"Are you pretending?"

Her eyes look so blank. She shakes her head.

I should have planned before I came over. Figured out the right words and brought more things to help her remember. I don't have anything to bring back the real Nia.

Except for me.

Nobody's watching. I look up at the windows that overlook the pool. The white blinds are drawn against the sun. Check again through the glass doors. Nobody.

I'm so sick of being careful.

So I step close to her and take her face between both my hands.

She freezes, her eyes big. But she doesn't say anything. Doesn't move.

I kiss her. Soft, slow, like our first kiss. For a second I feel her muscles give in. Everything relaxes. But she doesn't respond. Just sits, passive. Letting me do it.

It doesn't feel right. I'm not kissing my girl. She's a rubbery nothing.

Nia rips her lips away, turning her head to the side. "Stop that," she says, her voice shaking.

"You have to remember." I pull her head close with one hand, gentle, careful. And I kiss her again.

This time she takes a step back. "Respectful space in every place!"

She's really gone. All those tricks—the art, the chocolate, the lilacs—didn't really work. I only imagined something was left inside.

"Why don't you want me?" I ask. My face is wet. I'm crying, without even knowing. As soon as I notice, a sob rips through my gut. I grip my stomach.

"Are you sick?" She reaches out a hand, then pulls back. Touches her lips with the tips of her fingers.

"I love you," I tell her. "I have to save you."

"But there's nothing wrong with me." Now she's standing close, so close. She puts a light hand on my back. I feel the outline of each finger. "You're in pain. Do you need to sit down?"

Her voice is so sincere, so worried. It fools me for a second. She still cares. She still loves me. There's hope.

I straighten up and then our lips are together again.

She stops me with a hard shove. I'm staggering, spinning, trying to get my balance. The pool is coming but my legs can't save me. My body slaps into the water like I've been shot.

Nia stands over me, her arms crossed over her chest. Just stares. And blinks.

Water. I hate being in water. Does she remember? I lift a soggy arm, try to touch the side. But I can't.

I should ask for help. Demand the Styrofoam ring hanging behind her. But I feel heavy. Like trying to save myself would be wasted effort.

Besides, I'm worried about something else.

I'm floating on my back. Staring at her.

"Please don't tell," I say. As if I'm some normal Candor kid who cares what people think.

A thought whispers through my brain, like a Message. *Maybe you're just like the rest of them. Maybe you're not so special.*

Her mouth opens. Closes. I think of the fish my father caught, the day he told me to be her friend. But it was me who was hooked.

Then she says something. "All I want is to be good."

"You used to want things for yourself," I tell her. Like me.

"Don't touch me again."

All the Candor-installed remorse makes my mouth move. "I won't. I promise."

She just leaves. Walks inside the house and leaves me floating in the pool, arms wide like I'm making snow angels. Staring up at the sky.

The water tugs on my clothes. If I don't fight it, I'll sink. Pulled down to the bottom. It would be easy. Easier than making the few short strokes and big heave to get out of the water.

I've been fighting for eleven years. Maybe it's time to stop.

My clothes are getting heavier. Tugging against the body inside. I shut my eyes and let it happen. My legs go down first, with my sneakers pointing to the bottom. I'm upright, my chin touching the water. Then the tug is faster. I'm going under.

When the water reaches my nostrils, I know what I'll do.

I won't fight anymore.

But that doesn't mean I'm quitting.

I kick my legs and jerk my head up. Suck in air. New ideas flood my brain, like they've been waiting all my life.

No more helping people for money. No more hiding behind Mr. Perfect. I tried it. And I screwed up the one person who's loved me since my mother left.

The only way to fix things is to change everything.

I make the few heaving strokes to the side and pull myself out. Walk straight through their house, dripping water everywhere. Nobody is there. It's empty, but with light music playing, like a showroom of cheap furniture.

I don't call for Nia.

That's not how it's going to work now.

I just let myself out.

chapter 30

I CELEBRATE MY decision with the snooze button.

The alarm goes off at five, like always. Dark like all the others. Coffee waiting to be made. School after that.

I squint at the clock and look for the button. I've never used it before. I'll have a new kind of morning soon. I should practice.

I press the button.

Then it's six. Getting light out. Six. Six! Less than an hour before school. It's too late. I pushed things too far. Dad will be wondering why I'm not up. Hungry decaf Dad. I don't want to deal with that.

I throw on a polo. White socks. Khakis. I almost forget the post-card I wrote out last night. It's tucked in page 436 of my calc book. I pull it out and jam it into my back pocket.

It's our ticket out of town.

The smell of coffee meets me halfway down the steps. Morning music is already playing in the ceiling speakers.

I'm caught.

But he just smiles when he sees me. "About time."

The newspaper has that folded puffy look, like it's been read and put back together. His coffee cup has just a splash of brown in the bottom.

My hand slides to my back pocket before I can stop it. The card is still there, tucked low and safe. He can't see it.

"Good morning," I say. "You want more coffee?"

"Sit." He hooks the chair next to him with his foot and pulls it close. "We have some things to review."

Dad pushes aside the paper. There's a small device in front of him. It's about the size of a box of frozen peas. He slides it close, cradling it in both hands.

Sleeping in was stupid. Why was I in such a hurry to see how it would feel, being free? Now everything is different. And that's the opposite of what I need. For the next week, things have to stay normal. Nobody can suspect.

"You want toast? Orange juice?" I ask. Like I'm his waiter, not his kid. Like there's not some electronic gadget in front of him that's making me shake.

He pats the chair next to him and raises an eyebrow.

I sit.

He flips the top of the gadget open to reveal a video screen. I recognize it now. Some of the kids bring this device when they come here. You can play games. Check e-mail.

But nobody e-mails here, and the Messages take care of wanting to play games.

"Wow. What's that?" I do my best to sound awed. Curious.

He doesn't answer. Just thumbs a green button. Video starts playing.

It's me. Me, in my bathroom. Brushing my teeth. I'm shifting my weight from one foot to the other. Squinting at myself in the mirror. A little bit of drool escapes from my mouth.

It looks so normal. Except for the whole part about being taped.

"Remember, son. Thirty seconds each side, top and bottom," Dad says. "I see you doing twenty, tops."

"You taped me." I'm too shocked to try and figure out what I'm supposed to say.

"New security package. Got to test the products before selling."

My neck itches like someone's watching me. I look up at the ceiling, expecting to see a huge camera trained on my face. Tracking me everywhere. But there're just the usual speakers and the snake of designer lights.

Where'd he hide them?

Dad runs his finger over the screen and the video fast-forwards. I watch tiny Oscar finish getting ready for bed. Blue shorts with the stripes down the side. Gray Cubs T-shirt. I wore that last night.

Did he install the cameras yesterday?

Or were they always there?

Logic filters through my shock. Don't argue. He's acting like this is acceptable. Just your typical video-stalking of your teen. Not like he saw anything too shocking.

Now on-screen Oscar is sitting at his desk, doing homework. Dad fast-forwards and the pages of my history book fly by. My hand takes notes at a frantic pace.

My heart beats fast. Did he catch me writing out the postcard?

"Where is it?" he mutters. More fast-forwarding. "There."

The video slows to normal. I'm staring into space. Tapping a pencil eraser on my top teeth.

"I'm very disappointed," he says.

It hurts, and it irritates me, too. "I was thinking."

"I expect better than that." He snaps the screen shut and dips his chin to give me a stern stare over his nose. "Focus. Work. There's not a spot on your transcript for hours spent daydreaming."

"Sorry," I say. My eyes won't stop flicking to the video player. Is he done? Did he catch me, but he's not going to say anything?

When will I know for sure?

"We paid a lot of money for your dental work," he says.

"Thirty seconds each side," I say.

Dad checks his watch. "Ten minutes to school. Better hustle."

And I have to run my errand before I get to school. I wrap my rye toast in a paper towel and hurry to the NEV. At least he's not driving me to school. Not yet. Or maybe . . . maybe there's a video camera in here, too.

As soon as I'm away from the house, I pull over. No pinholes in the sun visor or the roof. I slide my fingers over the inside of the roof. No lumps, no wires—at least that I can feel. Maybe I'm safe.

Safe enough to take a risk. I have to do this—to save Nia and me. Before he figures things out.

Besides, once they fix Mandi, she might make more sense. If she can get past the psychotic biting thing. Then she might try to hurt me in other ways. Like telling.

I pull away from the curb and drive as fast as I dare. The parking lot behind the post office is empty. If I hurry, nobody will see me.

I slide the card out of my back pocket.

It's the last postcard I'll send to Frank. There's a photo of a dolphin on front, like always. A speech bubble pokes out of its open mouth. *Making a splash in Florida*, it reads.

I double-check the message I wrote.

PU 02:15 Site 2 10/18

Pickup at 2:15 A.M. at Site 2, on October 18.

We're leaving, Nia and me. It gives me one week to get everything ready.

Including Nia.

I pull open the metal door to the mailbox and set the postcard inside. Then I let the door slam shut.

Just to be sure, I open the door and peek.

The postcard is gone.

My plan is officially under way.

chapter 31

GETTING NIA TO leave with me will be the hardest part. I rushed in. It was stupid. Now she thinks I'm a rude jerk. Not that she's wrong. It's just she used to like that jerk.

I'll have to use the Messages on her, one last time. Just to get her to understand what she has to do.

But I'll need help. Listening to my new CD will have to be someone else's idea. Someone trustworthy.

Someone I can control.

Mandi's not an option. She'll be away for a while. And dangerous when she comes back.

That leaves Sherman. I fed him a few Messages with his last batch. He should want to help.

I position myself at the start of the lunch line, holding two trays. A few minutes later, Sherman shows up. He's counting change in his hand like a kid who broke open his piggy bank.

"I'm hungry," he moans.

For once I'm happy to see him. "Lunch is my treat," I tell him. "Get whatever you want."

"Healthy bodies make strong minds." He sighs and runs a chubby finger over the change in his palm.

"Then I'll get you a double order of applesauce."

"No thanks. I have enough money for what I'm supposed to eat. My mother counted it out this morning." Sherman takes the tray and trudges into line.

Why am I bothering? I don't have to bribe him. I own him.

"I could use some help," I tell him.

A smile breaks over his face. "I am Oscar's helper."

"But it has to be a secret."

His face twitches. "Secrets are bad. I'm not supposed to talk about secrets anymore. Never keep secrets from your family. Secrets are—"

"I got it." Looks like Dad delivered nice new booster Messages to the Golub home after Mandi's escape attempt. And Sherman did a thorough job listening. Will it block my own Messages? Or twist them the wrong way?

It actually might make me safer. Now I don't have to worry about Sherman stealing the CD for himself.

Of course, he still might squeal.

Maybe I have to offer him something else to make him do what I want. But what?

"Want to sit with me?" Sherman's smile is still pathetic. He's not the full Candor model yet, confident in his specialness.

"For a little bit, maybe—"

"Oh, good. Mandi's out sick, and everybody else keeps asking me to sit with them, but"—Sherman plops down at a table for two— "I'd rather hang out with you."

Now I know what I can give him.

Me.

It won't be easy. But it's just seven days. And it's for Nia.

"Maybe we could sit together at study hall, too," I say.

He stops chewing and stares at me with happy puppy eyes. "Like best friends?"

"Best friends." For the next seven days, at least.

"Me and Oscar Banks best friends. Wow." Sherman shakes his head.

"That's right. And you know what best friends do?" I ask.

Sherman's eyes slide to his food. Then he slowly looks up at me. "Share food?" he whispers. "I mean . . . I *am* worthy."

That Message was a dud. It made Mandi run and Sherman get fatter.

"You're right. Friends do share food." I slide over my cardboard tub of carrots.

His fingers hover over them.

"They're good for you," I tell him.

He shoves two in his mouth. Chomps down. Orange flecks slide out of the corner of his mouth.

"Friends help each other with things, too," I say.

"I am Oscar's helper," he repeats.

I slide the envelope out of my notebook. "Can you give this to someone for me?"

This is my biggest risk. Another CD. In Sherman's hands. He could steal it. Or listen to it—which would demolish my whole plan.

But I can't think of a better way to do this.

Sherman nods, still chewing. At least the Messages save me from seeing him talk with his mouth full.

"You can't tell her that it's from me. And you have to slip it to her in school. No home delivery."

He moans. "That's a secret."

"Don't worry. It's not a secret. It's a surprise. Just make sure she listens."

"I like surprises." Sherman takes the envelope and peeks inside. "Who's it for?"

"Nia Silva."

He grins and wiggles his eyebrows. "Are they love songs? Can I make a copy for Mandi?"

"Bad idea." I make a grab, but he's fast—it's in his backpack already. "No sharing. It's just for Nia."

"Fine."

"Promise me," I order.

He rolls his eyes. "I promise. She'll get it today."

Things have flipped. Used to be Sherman needed me. Now I'm the one begging. If he screws up, my whole plan is wrecked.

Our escape depends on Sherman. The guy who paid me to get out and got stuck staying instead.

"You sure I can't buy you something else? An apple or . . . whatever?" I ask.

"Want to go to the movies with me? It's a new cartoon." His hand slides into his backpack, like he's touching the envelope. Maybe he's thinking of how I owe him.

"Sure," I say. "That's what best buds do, right?"

"We can go to the matinee after school."

"I can't wait." My last movie in Candor.

Sherman stands up and gives me a knowing smile. "I'd better go do my special delivery."

"Bye." I watch him walk out of the cafeteria. To find Nia? Or to do something I don't want him to do?

Trusting him is a bad idea. I know it. It's always safest to trust yourself.

But I can't do this alone.

And I don't have any better options.

chapter **32**

SAVING NIA MEANS breaking the first promise I ever made.

After Mom left and Dad smashed all her art, he took me to the new ice-cream parlor.

Ice cream was for celebrations, not sad things. But I wasn't turning it down. I remember standing in front of the case at Dairymen's. Forty flavors were lined up in a double row.

"I want pistachio chip," I told the tall woman behind the counter. It wasn't what I was supposed to order. The full-fat, full-of-sugar flavors at Dairymen's are for the tourists. The Candor people are supposed to slide to the right and pick from the healthy flavors at the end of the case.

Her eyes flicked to Dad. I looked, too. He frowned, but then he gave her a tiny nod. "Give me the coffee frozen yogurt," he said.

We took our cones outside. It was hot. My legs stuck to the wicker chair, and I peeled them up, slow, my skin glued to the grid of the seat.

My pistachio chip didn't taste like much. But it was cold and I wanted to pretend everything was okay. Good, even. So I ate it. I bit off pieces. Licking it would take too long.

"Everyone leaves," Dad told me then. It was the first time he ever said it.

"I won't," I told him.

No reply. He stared across the street at the pond he'd named after my mother. Lake Lulu. His nickname for her.

I took a big crunchy bite of the cone. The sharp edges scraped the inside of my lip.

Dad held his cone high and near his face. It looked like he was about to lick it. But he didn't. Just let it melt. It ran over his fingers and dropped to the ground.

"I promise I'll never leave," I said.

He didn't say anything. But I'd promised out loud.

He warned me a lot after that: everyone leaves. I always made the same promise that I'd stay. At first I said it out loud. Sometimes he'd smile and say something vague, like, "That's nice." But mostly he didn't reply.

After a while I made the promise in my head instead.

I wanted to show him he was wrong, maybe. That I could be trusted—I was different from Winston, from Mom.

But now I'm going to prove he was right. Everyone leaves. Even me.

Maybe I'm supposed to feel sad, or guilty. But I don't. Nia changed me, and then he changed Nia. I'm not the boy who made those promises.

I don't owe him anything.

Still, I need to say good-bye. He's still my father. No matter how much I hate what he'd built Candor—and himself—into.

But he can't know it's good-bye until after I'm gone.

So I ask him out for ice cream one more time, after dinner.

"Why?" he asks.

"Because I want to."

Simple truth. It surprises him. He shifts his jaw from side to side. Then he picks up his NEV keys. "Fine."

This time I order the fat-free sugar-free cup of good-boy blah. But I get strawberries on mine. Sugary limp strawberries with red juice that pools in the bottom of the clear plastic cup.

"At least it has lots of vitamin D," I say. An apology, like even fruit is a dangerous indulgence.

Dad shakes his head but he doesn't say anything. I lead him to the same outside table where we sat on our first day as a family of two. The wicker chairs have been replaced since then. And the trees around Lake Lulu are taller now.

We eat without talking.

I want to know what will happen when I leave. I know some things for sure: he'll send out people to look for me. And eventually he'll use the Messages to make people forget I ever existed.

But how will he feel? Will he choose to forget me, too?

"Will you miss me when I go to Yale?" I ask.

Like all those years ago, his eyes are glued to the lake. "You'll be home for the holidays."

"It'll be quiet without me, right?" Maybe as quiet as it was after Winston was gone. The house was silent. All I could hear was my breathing. I hated the sound. I hated me, hogging all the oxygen, when Winston didn't have any, didn't need any.

"I'll manage." Dad shrugs.

Still, I can't help pushing. In four more days, I'm gone. I want to know how much it will hurt.

Because part of me thinks I'll miss him a lot.

"What if I stay away?" I ask. "I could go to a friend's house for Christmas."

A small confident smile parts his mouth. His lips are coated in vanilla frozen yogurt, the liquid settling in the lines. "Children always come home to Candor, sooner or later."

The same words are in my brain, waves reminding me in an even rhythm. A Message that everyone hears and believes.

Pretty soon Candor will have a lot of overambitious kids with fancy degrees, wanting to move back in with Mommy and Daddy.

But the right Message can fix almost anything. He'll figure it out.

"I'll miss you," I say. Trying to keep it casual. But having to say it.

"You'll be fine," Dad says. He scrapes his spoon around the bottom of the cup, getting every last bit.

I'll miss fooling him. Being perfect when I choose it but letting him think he made me that way. But I won't miss the fear. The wondering: What if he finds out? What will he do? Will my brain survive it?

"I'll be fine," I tell Dad. "I know I will be."

We don't stay long. There's not much to talk about. He's got work to do.

And I've got an escape to get ready for.

chapter 33

MOST PEOPLE PACK when they're leaving.

Not me. Everything I'll need is waiting outside. I have a fat off-shore bank account—which wasn't easy to get. The first kid I asked to set it up stole all my money. But the second kid did his job. Now I have a pile of green security ready for me.

And my clients are in every major city, grateful. Ready to help in any way. They'll get us fake IDs. Disguises. A place to live.

I don't have to pack. I have to destroy what I'm leaving behind, so nobody can follow us or find us.

Getting past Dad's cameras is boring and takes too long. I just tell my new best friend, Sherman, what to do.

The phone rings just as it's getting dark—exactly the time I told him. "Can you come over and study?" he asks.

Dad is staring. "Sherman doesn't understand the Krebs Citric Acid Cycle," I explain.

He takes the phone. "Let me talk to his parents."

They make the appropriate adult noises and he lets me leave.

When I get to the shed, I pull open the door to my stash. The faint, familiar smell wafts out: chocolate and the oiliness of electronics gear stuffed in close quarters.

First I pull out the magazines. Rip the pages and crumple into balls. Pile in the middle of the floor.

Good tinder.

Next come the electronics. They won't burn like paper. But if the fire's hot enough, they should melt. Nobody will know what the plastic blobs used to be.

But I jump on them, just to be sure. Crack them into pieces beneath my feet. DVD players. Games. The blank CDs I used for all my Messages. I've made the ones for our escape already.

I don't need these things anymore.

Even Nia's museum goes in the pile. I'll take her to see the real paintings soon.

Then I pull out the one bottle of liquor that's left. And some gasoline, the real stuff, left from the gardeners who mow the lawn. One of the ribbons hanging from the rafters makes a decent wick.

I jam the stopper back in the bottle and take one last look. My secret place. The one place where I didn't have to be perfect. I brought clients here. Then I sent them away.

Are they happy? I've never wondered before.

I step into the yard and lift the lighter, but then I see a shadow by the pool. A person-shaped shadow, sitting, watching me.

Flick the lighter off. Set the bottle down slowly, slowly, behind a bush. Get ready to run.

The shadow stands up and comes toward me, graceful and tall.

"Nia?" It comes out too quiet for her to hear.

She stops close to me, closer than polite. Lifts a single finger and lays it over my lips. It's soft and warm.

Sherman really gave her the CDs. I didn't realize how nervous I was until now. Joy fills me, sudden and hot.

This plan will actually work.

"The TAG patrol is coming back soon," Nia whispers. Her finger falls off my lip. "You'd better hurry."

There's a badge gleaming on her chest. "Aren't you the patrol?"

"Yes. And I'd better start doing my job soon."

"Why are you here?" I ask. "To bust me?"

"You told me you would be here when I was ready."

She was listening. Joy fills me. Makes me brave. "Do you remember?" I ask.

She comes even closer. Her breath brushes my cheek. "Some things."

My Messages have certain instructions.

Where and when to meet me the night we leave. That she can't tell anybody. And to meet me here, if she can.

She's coming back to life, all because of my Messages. The ones she hated me for giving her, before. The reason we broke up.

We have to leave before she realizes what I've done. I'll explain after we're gone. Maybe in the real world she'll understand.

Or at least not leave me.

"Will you be there?" I ask.

She nods. I put my hand on her cheek and lean in. This time she won't throw me in the pool.

But she jumps back. "What are you doing?"

She's not all changed—not yet.

"I have to finish something. Stay here." I go back to the bush and pull out the bottle. Walk back to where she's standing, watching. Her hands are tucked in her back pockets, her elbows sticking out on either side like wings.

She should leave. What if she gets the urge to tell?

"Can I light it?" Nia asks.

"How did you know what I'm doing?" I ask.

"I think I used to do bad things," she whispers. "A long time ago."

I never want to tell her no again, but my hand spasms around the bottle. This is something I have to do.

"Next time," I tell her.

She laughs. Too loud: it echoes off the pool, the brick pavers. Announces we're here.

"Step back. Go back to the pool and be ready to run."

"I remember swimming with you," she says. "But not here. Was it real?"

"Yes." I smile, remembering that night. "You made me do it."

"You made me do things, too—didn't you?"

"I'm sorry." I'm still controlling her. But I can't tell her now.

"It wasn't all bad." Her voice is low, sexy. I reach out to touch her, but she turns away. Walks to edge of the pool and stands at the edge. Watching.

The pool is my emergency exit. If things go faster than I think, I'll—we'll—dive in there. I hate swimming, but I hate bursting into flames even more.

It won't take long for the fire trucks to come. Dad built Candor its own fire station, just in case. Probably this wasn't the fire he was worried about.

But Dad's always ready for anything to happen.

I hold the bottle high and away from my face. Check the wick. It's wet. Waiting.

One flick of the lighter and the wick is burning. I hurl it into the middle of the shed. It lands right in the middle of my pile. Liquid fire flies in every direction.

It's done.

I should run. Follow the plan. But now that I've done it, I realize it hurts. I'm burning a friend. The place that hid me and let me be real.

And there's no going back.

"I'm sorry," I whisper.

There's still our place in the woods. I won't touch that. It'll stay out there, hidden. Even if someone finds it, they won't see the memories we made there.

The flames are spreading now, crawling along the liquid gas trails I left behind. Smoke is coming off the shingles. The inside of the shed glows orange, like an oven.

I hear sirens. "Come on!" Nia shouts. The fence slams shut. She's gone.

Something ugly crawls into me. Anger? Jealousy? She left without me. Shouldn't we have stayed together?

No. She's safe. That's what matters.

Even if it hurts me.

One last look and I finally turn to go.

There's nothing left now except for running.

chapter 34

I GET HOME without seeing anybody, taking alleys and boardwalks through the woods. The fire trucks zoom down the main streets, their red lights bouncing between houses to light up the pavement I'm walking on.

Lights flick on in houses when the sirens come close. I imagine everyone rushing to their front windows—away from the windows where they could look out and see me.

We don't get a lot of fires in Candor—brainwashed people tend to be good about fire safety, if they're told to be. This will be the event of the week—maybe even the month.

Dad's NEV is gone when I get home. I walk right in the front door. Safe.

Then I remember. There are cameras everywhere. Now I'm on tape, coming in after curfew. Almost an hour past it.

I could try to make excuses. Studying ran late. I stopped to watch the fire trucks. Pretty red lights distract me.

But there's no room for suspicion. Not now. I want this to be an easy, clean getaway. Don't need Dad making things hard.

I have to find that video. And destroy it.

It's not in the wire closet where the rest of the house equipment is. But I know where to look: Dad hides everything in his study.

There's a new filing cabinet next to his desk. It's locked. But that's not a problem. I borrow the nail file from his top desk drawer and I'm in.

The drawer holds a small black box. It's the same one he showed me the other morning. But that's all. No wires, no tapes, no central command system. When something is that simple, it's hard to believe it's dangerous.

I settle into the giant leather chair in the corner, by the electric fireplace. The cushions feel stiff, like he's never had time to use it.

"Showtime," I whisper. Then I flip the screen up and watch.

It's all on there. Six sections, one for each camera. I check the one labeled FRONT. And there I am, walking in the door with a big stupid grin on my face. I practically skip toward the camera until I've escaped its range.

I switch to the KITCHEN section. It picks up where the other left off. I look nervous in the video. It's easy to tell I'm worried.

There's a section for my bedroom, my bathroom, and the hallway. But two places don't have video: Dad's bedroom and the study. Guess he thinks he doesn't need monitoring. Besides, who'd watch it?

Nobody ever checks to see if Dad is being naughty.

But I could.

How long do I have? There aren't any sirens outside anymore. It's been a while. He could come home soon. And if he catches me here, with his box . . .

I'd miss my appointment with Frank. Too busy having my brain turned to goo.

Five minutes. I'll see if I can catch him being bad—or just human—for five minutes. Then I'll erase my part and be done.

I'll have to find him somewhere with cameras, alone. I slide my thumb and watch the week slide by. It's a lot of empty house, and some of me. I find a few shots of Dad reading his paper. Sipping his coffee. Flip the page. Sip. Flip.

"How do you like being spied on?" I ask the screen. But there's nothing private. Not like me brushing my teeth or being alone in my room. I want something more.

Then I remember: his study is next to the front entry and he leaves his door open sometimes. Talks loud on the phone.

I might be able to hear him.

Slide to last night. I made turkey cutlets. He ate. I washed dishes. He went to his study. I remember I could hear him blabbing about gas prices and lawn mowers on the phone.

The hall is empty in the video. I turn the volume up. Dad got the fancy kind of surveillance: there's even sound.

"Doubling their rates!" Dad's fake-o Southern twang echoes a little, but it's clear. Too loud, even.

"Have to look elsewhere . . . people don't want their fees going up . . ." Boring.

Wonder what he said when they called him about my little fire? I'll bet that was loud enough to pick up. I jump to the video from tonight. There's me again. Rewind. An empty hall.

"So it was a routine inspection?" Dad's voice. Quieter.

Silence, like he's listening to someone on the phone. Then mumbling. I adjust the volume again.

"You got the little bastard. Er, brat." Dad's voice is so loud I think he's in the room with me. I hit pause.

Who's he talking about, and what'd they do? The only bad thing in Candor is me. Did Dad find out about the graffiti? Or worse—my CDs?

He could be here any second. How long does it take to put a fire out and tell people not to worry?

Not long enough. It's dumb to be sitting here, doing this.

But I can't stop now. I want to know what he's talking about. And I'm good at making excuses. I can handle him if he catches me.

So I watch some more.

"A dozen? And they all said the same thing?"

My CDs. He found my CDs. My stomach is burning. I gag.

"Must have ripped them out of the notebook and tossed them," Dad says. "Odd that your staff didn't catch the kid writing that stuff."

No. It's not the CDs. But what?

Dad laughs, so loud the speakers make a metallic buzz. "Handwriting analysis won't be necessary."

Silence, every second making me sweat. When you're the only bad boy in town, it's a good guess any catching will involve you.

"We'll just meet them there. They gave us directions." Laughing again, so hard that he must be crying. "Mile marker two-forty-seven on Thursday morning. It couldn't be easier."

Those are my directions. The ones I fed to Nia in the Messages.

She's the only one who knows them besides me. And I haven't been writing them down anywhere.

She's betrayed me.

Dad is still talking. "Don't worry, Charles. Once we fix this kid, we've fixed the town."

He knows. Not everything—but enough.

"Good job on this," Dad says. "Now the rest is up to us. We're going hunting on Thursday."

The only safe thing to do is to stay. I'll be alone again. Stuck seeing the shell of the one girl who loved the real me.

Headlights through the window. Dad's home.

I panic. There's a reformat command on the player. I make the selection and toss it back in the drawer. Race into the hallway and to the kitchen.

The door opens ten seconds later. He's home.

And I'm stuck here with him.

chapter 35

TWO DAYS LATER. Midnight.

Everything is ready. A backpack with two players, loaded with the right Messages. Food. Water. Enough of everything to get us out safely.

But Nia ruined everything.

She probably didn't mean to do it. I pushed so many Messages in her brain, they had to come out somewhere. So she put them on paper.

Paper they found.

If I leave the house, Dad's cameras will catch it.

But it's Thursday. I can't stay here. She knows where to go, what time to be there. My Messages will get her caught.

I won't let that happen.

Beep-beep-beep. Slam.

Dad's left the house. I look out the window. He's halfway to his NEV, moving fast. He can't wait to catch his special someone. That kid who's been messing with his perfect product.

It's too late to get ahold of our ride, to tell him to come later or sooner or another day. He'll be there, at 2:15.

Dad will be there, waiting. He and his loyal employees, hunting.

But they won't catch us. I'll find a way to get us out.

We'll go to a safe place where Nia can heal. Eventually she'll remember who she really is.

There's only one path to our meeting place. I go quick and quiet. If anyone's lurking, I'll hear it.

But there's nobody except me. They must be doing this the easy way. Just waiting where Nia's paper told them to go.

I get to the hunting stand. A wood platform is nailed high in the trees, with wood slats leading up to it. Hunters—the real kind—put it there, years before Dad made Candor. They'd sit for hours and watch. Hoping for one clean shot.

It's cool out tonight. I wish I brought my sweatshirt for Nia.

The woods are quiet. No frogs singing tonight. Too cold for them, I guess. Maybe they're hibernating. Or maybe they're dead.

Something streaks past me, so close I could touch it. I duck low. But then I hear a long squeak down on the ground. It was an owl. More hunting. A mouse dying.

At least the owl does it to survive.

Then I see someone's head, covered, bobbing down the path. The leaves rattle. If it's Nia, she's not good at being quiet. Or she doesn't know how dangerous this is.

The person stops and looks around, then pushes her hood back.

It's Nia. My breath goes short and unsteady while I watch.

She lets her ponytail loose and shakes it free. Then she tugs it back into place. I'm holding my breath, watching her. She pulls the hood back on.

I squat and grab the edge of the platform and swing myself down to the ground. A splinter stabs my finger. The pain surprises me.

She's running. Running away from me. Running to where she's supposed to be.

"No!" I risk shouting it, but she doesn't stop.

We race down the path. She's fast, too fast. One tree root or stone and I'll wipe out. Did I scare her? Or is she just in a hurry?

She stops.

We're here. The last place I wanted to be.

I stop before she can see me. Listen in the shadows.

I don't think anyone is here yet. But it won't be long.

"It's me," I say in a low voice.

She slowly turns around. I can see her teeth glowing in a smile. It's not perky. It's the real Nia, sly, looking like she's about to do something dirty. "This was your idea?" she asks.

"It was the only way."

"I remember more now." She takes fast, broad steps until she's with me in the dark. "I think I hate you."

But then she presses her body against mine and lays a kiss on me. Full-on, wet, warm.

It's all I've wanted since we split. I fold her into me. Show her how much I've missed her. There's the smell of lilacs. The taste of mint and raspberries and salt. Everything is how it's supposed to be.

She talks with her lips still against mine. "We used to do this in the woods, didn't we?"

"We did." I pull back. I want more. But not now. "We're leaving."

Her eyes go wide. Then they slide to the backpack. "Now I understand."

"A truck is picking us up." I push the bag into her hands. "You'll go first."

That's my big plan. Running like hell. It's not much. But I can't change where the truck will pick us up. And I can't stop my father from being there. All we can do is be faster than him.

She holds the backpack out, halfway between us, like she doesn't want to take it.

"Why should I go?" she asks.

"Because you want to." I made sure of that with my Messages.

She nods. "I'll go."

I knew she would.

"Run like the woods are on fire. Don't wait for me. I'll see you on the truck."

"Promise?" she asks. Her voice wobbles like a little girl's.

"Promise."

There's the sound of a motor. Someone is coming down the road. Five minutes too soon.

"Get down." I fall to my knees. She hesitates.

I grab her sweatshirt and pull until she's on the ground, too.

"Why are we hiding? Aren't we supposed to run?" she asks.

"I have to make sure it's the right truck."

Headlights splash the trees at the edge of the road. Brighter. Brighter. And then the truck pulls into view.

The white truck with the Candor crest.

It's sitting still now. Waiting.

When Frank pulls up, they'll pounce. We're done.

Unless . . . unless they catch someone. They're not looking for two people.

Only one.

"Can we go?" Nia whispers.

"No." I hold my finger to my lips, barely breathe the words. "It's a trap."

Her eyes narrow. "How do you know?"

"My father got a phone call. They know someone is running," I say.

"There's no way—"

"You told them."

I watch her face. Wait to see guilt, realization, or something.

But she just looks confused. "But I didn't even know I was running away until now. I didn't tell anybody."

"You wrote it down."

"This place." Nia's head drops low. "It was filling my head. But I threw it away. I never put my name on it."

"Listen to me," I say. "When I tell you, run. Get in the other truck that's coming—not the white one. Go in the one with the alligator on the side."

"But the white one—"

"Is my problem."

I'll save her. Because I love her. Because I want to show her she's worth it.

I love her more than I want to be safe.

She shakes her head. But she lets me put the headphones on her head. "Press play as soon as he pulls away. Don't stop listening. Ever. Got it?"

"I can survive here," Nia says. Her long fingertips touch the headphones lightly.

"No. You wouldn't be you. Which is as good as dead."

Nia tilts her head up and stares at the sky.

"The only way to survive is to leave," I tell her.

"I'll come back if you don't make it," she says. "I'll save you."

"Don't. They'll catch you." My voice is more certain than I feel. Giving myself up temporarily is one thing. But forever?

I don't feel ready for forever. But at least I won't know I'm gone.

"Don't ever come back," I tell her. "Promise."

She drags her backpack onto her shoulders, lifting it like it weighs a hundred pounds. Slow and painful.

"I can't promise," she says.

"I love you," I tell her.

She doesn't say it back. It's okay. She'll remember eventually. After she's left.

There's another set of headlights. Driving slow. Stopping fifteen, maybe twenty feet behind the white van.

The white van's side door slides open, slowly.

"Run!" I give her a shove. *"Now!"*

Then I turn on my flashlight and head the other way, straight to the white van.

Everyone leaves. Everyone except me. I guess I'm meant to stay.

It's the only way anyone else can escape.

chapter 36

THEY HAVE TO see me before they see Nia. Before they can stop Frank from driving away with her.

I flick my flashlight around. Wild, crazy. Like I'm a shipwrecked sailor signaling the ship offshore. See me. Save me. Take me home.

The light bounces off the jagged palm leaves and shines in their windows.

Nia's running, flying almost as fast as if she's on her board. I remember how she raced away from me that first night. How I listened to her wheels rumble, farther and farther away. Then it was quiet.

She was smart to leave me then. She's even smarter now.

The van has a green circle on the side. The Candor seal. All the windows in the back are up high and dark.

The rear door slides open. I can't hear it—the only sound in my ears is Nia's feet, crunching over dead leaves, and her breath, loud, desperate.

She's almost there. A shadow stands by her van. Frank, waiting for her.

I swing the light straight into their eyes.

"There!" A tall thick man jumps out of the van and heads for me. He doesn't look over by Nia.

I hear a door slam.

Frank's van is pulling away.

Arms reach out through the dark. They drag me inside the van. I don't fight it. But they throw me on the metal floor anyway. It's dark inside. There's grit on my cheek. The smell of fertilizer makes me gag.

"Got him!" the man yells.

Someone shoves my wrists together. There's a zipping sound. Handcuffs? I try to pull free but I'm stuck.

"Who was that?" another voice says. "The other car?"

"Maybe a lost tourist."

"Maybe not."

The voices blend together. They all mean the same thing to Nia. Danger.

I can't let them wonder. They can't follow. Can't stop her from getting away.

I make my hands shake. Then my legs, straight, stiff, toes hammering against the floor. Finally my head. I bang my forehead against the metal. Again. Again.

"The ants! The ants!" I scream. "They're in my ears! Get them out!"

"Better go. Brat's seeing things." A man's voice. His shoes are next to my face, I think. The door to the van slides shut and now it's completely dark.

"I'll make him see things." A bright ball of light, shining. Someone grabs my hair and drags my head up. The flashlight is in my eyes now, but all I see is pain. I will myself not to blink.

"Do you see them? Get them!" I scream. "They're biting!"

"There's nothing there," a voice says. "So shut up."

Behind me someone speaks. "Give him the juice. I'll hold and you stick him."

"Can't." The light goes out and the man drops my head. I let it fall heavy to the floor. "Boss man's up front, remember?"

My father. Up front. Something surges through my stomach. I don't know if I'm afraid or excited. What will he do when he sees me?

The van swerves and bumps. The men are quiet now. Waiting, I guess. Saving their energy for where we're going.

They probably think I'll fight it.

The van stops. A square of light shows on the wall over my head. Dad's face looks in.

Everything is about to change.

"I want to see," he says. "Which lucky parent gets the call?"

I try to stand up. But I'm dizzy. And there's something wet running down my cheeks, in my eyes. It's hard to see.

One of my buddies grabs the cuffs around my wrist and hauls me up. The plastic bites into the soft spot between my wrist and the bones of my hand. The pain clears my head.

"Oscar." He whispers it. Not like a question. More like an answer.

He stares at me. I stare back.

"My little boy," he says.

All this time I've wondered what I would say if he caught me. I'd beg him to understand. Or I'd tell him how alone I was. Because of him. He tried to push Winston out of my head. And he made Mom leave.

But only one thing comes out. "I got sick of rye toast."

A sour look twists his face. He turns to face the front. "Take him to the Room. Now."

The van starts moving again. Away from Nia. It worked.

Nia is safe.

I'm still scared. Not for her, not anymore. But now I see what's coming for me. And there's no escape left.

Dad's loyal henchman yanks me back to the floor of the van.

Pushes me with his foot until I'm lying down again, tasting metal and fertilizer grains.

"That hurt, asshole," I say loudly.

But my father doesn't turn around.

"You won't even remember that," the man hisses in my ear.

I know he's right. I'll be lucky if I remember my favorite flavor of Jell-O when they're done with me.

"It's wrong, Dad," I say. "You have to stop. People should think for themselves."

The little door slides shut and it's dark again.

A new feeling comes over me. It feels like heat. And cold. I want to scream, cry, even bite something.

It's rage. Different from anything I've felt in Candor. Different, even, from the time I almost pounded Sherman's face into the ground.

There hasn't been room for it, and soon it will be gone again.

Now is the only time I can let it rule me.

"I had a brother," I tell the darkness.

Nobody replies.

I say it louder. "I had a brother!"

Nothing.

"Listen to me!" I shout. I know he can hear me, even if the door is shut.

"I never forgot him!" And then I draw in breath to push out the loudest part yet. "His name was Winston Campbell Banks!"

The van is going faster now. It hugs a corner and I slide until my knee hits the side of the van. It hurts enough to drain me. My body tingles all over, blood beating in my ears and drying on my face.

"I wanted to be just like him," I croak. "Except that he's dead."

One of the men finally speaks. "Oscar Banks is an only child." He says it like a reminder. "Oscar Banks never had any siblings."

"My father fixed everything except me," I say. The man doesn't answer. But I didn't expect him to. "But now he wins."

The van stops moving.

When the door slides open, it's Dad on the other side. I stay on the floor, watching him, waiting to see what he'll do.

There's no hurry. Now all my time belongs to him.

"I never suspected," he says.

There's not much left to say. My tongue slides against the rough metal. It tastes like blood. "I never wanted you to."

"Cut his handcuffs."

My hands are free. The man helps me stand up. I see them now. Two men, shorter than I thought, wearing white coveralls. They're stained with green streaks. Gardeners helping to hunt runaways.

"If he let you decide, would you like your job?" I ask one of them.

He looks at the floor, where he shoved my face into it.

Dad holds out his hand. I take it. Our hands fit together. I remember my first day of school. Winston's funeral. Times when I trusted him to lead me.

One more time.

The night air feels warmer than it should. No breeze. Just heat and moist air covering my nostrils. It's hard to breathe.

I straighten my spine and let him lead me inside. I know I won't remember much when I leave. No Winston. No mother, maybe. Even the shed will be erased.

But Nia will be out there. Getting stronger every day. Becoming real again. Whatever happens, she won't forget.

As long as she remembers us, I'll still exist.

chapter 37

"I HAVE A special treat." Dad is smiling at me. He's hiding his hands behind his back.

There are only ten pages left in my chemistry chapter. I want to finish, but I mark the page and look up at him. Always strive to please your parents.

"When receiving a gift, it's the thought that counts," I tell him.

His smile is wide. "You make me proud, son."

It makes me feel like a sunny day. "Always strive to be your very best."

Then he shows me what he's holding. It's a clear glass vase filled with purple flowers. "They're lilacs," he says. "Smell them."

The flowers are made up of lots of tiny buds. I touch one with my fingertip before I inhale.

Have I done something wrong? He's staring at me. I pull back, but then he smiles. I feel better.

He sets them on my desk. "You talked in your sleep last night. You asked for these."

"I don't remember." I take another deep breath. My room usually smells like peaches and cucumbers. Now it smells like perfume.

Dad pulls a small notepad from his back pocket. He flips to a fresh page and writes something in it.

"The fever made me forget things," I tell him. Dad brought me here, to the hospital, when I got sick. It's been a few weeks, I think. I'm not sure. I don't know how to tell how long it's been.

"You might not ever remember everything," he says.

"It's okay," I say. "You'll tell me what I need to know." Parents always know what's best for their children.

He folds his arms and looks at me. "Do you like the flowers?"

"They're nice. Thank you for the present." I know that's what I'm supposed to say. But I wish he'd take them away. I like it better when my room smells like summer.

"You don't have to be polite, Oscar. Tell me if you really like the flowers."

Pain streaks across my forehead. It's the start of another headache. I get them all the time. Every single one surprises me.

Dad's face changes to his worried look. "Do you need your medicine?"

My hands are shaking again. I nod.

The fever damaged my nerves. I will always get headaches. But maybe they'll be better someday.

The pills taste bitter on my tongue. I swallow quickly, but the burning taste stays. "Will you please take the flowers away?" I ask. "They make my head hurt. I'm sorry."

"Of course." Dad doesn't look offended. He's even smiling.

Dad picks up the vase in both hands and looks up at the ceiling. My door opens with a hissing sound.

I don't follow him. When it's time to go outside, they'll tell me. Usually I go in the morning. I like to sit in the sun and watch the lizards race across the courtyard. Sometimes I bring my homework outside, too.

Spring midterms are coming up. I have to catch up with my

classmates. When I was very sick, I couldn't study. Now I'm doing better. I want to get straight As. Academics are the key to success.

The door hisses again. Dad is back. He's holding a clipboard. "Let's do your daily questions."

"I'll do better today." When I get all the questions right, it means my brain has healed from the fever. Then I can go home.

Dad sits in the cushy white chair that's opposite the bed. "Ice cream is . . ."

"A special treat. One must be careful to maintain a balanced diet." I always get that one right.

He nods and asks the next question without looking at the clipboard. "When you go on a date, should you hold a girl's hand?"

I shake my head. "Respectful space in every place."

"Good job. Let's skip to a new one." He runs his finger down the clipboard and stops near the bottom. Then he takes a deep breath. "What would you tell someone who wants to leave Candor?"

"Is there a field trip?"

"This is different. They want to leave for a long time, maybe even forever."

I can tell he's rooting for me. Dad wants me to give him the right answer. Parents always work to make their children succeed.

I wish I knew what I'm supposed to say.

"People don't leave Candor," I tell him.

"But what if someone wanted to?"

"I guess . . ." I look around my room. Everything is so clean and soft. Usually it's easy to think here, but my brain isn't working right now. "I guess I'd buy them a good-bye present?"

Dad lets out a soft sigh. He writes something on the board.

I know what that means. I've failed again. I hate being wrong. "Give me another one, please? I want to try again."

"You're not ready." Dad stands up and tucks the clipboard under his arm.

"Tell me how to study. I want to get better."

Dad shakes his head. "Just listen to the music, Oscar. Let your body heal. You're getting better every day."

"I want to be better now." I shouldn't sulk, but sometimes I hate being broken.

"Soon you'll be back at school. You'll finish the year and then you'll go to college. All of this will seem far away."

"I'll study hard. I'm going to Yale."

"Or maybe somewhere closer. We'll see." Dad pushes the hair off my forehead with his thumb, his fingers cupping my cheek. I close my eyes. It makes me remember being little. It's always been just the two of us, since the day he adopted me.

"I'll make you proud," I promise.

"We'll make sure of that, won't we?" Dad smiles like he's very proud of me. "See you at bedtime."

After he leaves, I pull out my notepad. I write down the questions he asked me, with the answers. I'll study them every two hours. I'll stare at them until I know every single answer.

Eventually I will get everything right.

Then they will let me leave here. I can go back to being a normal Candor kid. I will make my father proud. I will be a model citizen.

I will make sure everything is perfect.

Acknowledgments

MOM AND DAD, thank you for boosting my every endeavor and buying the TRS-80 that I wrote my first (blessedly lost) novel on. Pattyri, first fan and dearest friend, thanks for the tough reads and good questions—and for never letting me quit.

JASON, I'D TELL you your days of dishwashing are over, but you'd know I was lying. There are lots of books left in me. Thank you for giving me the time and space I need to put them on paper. And then you are there, waiting, when I need commiseration and love.

AS FOR THOSE friends and family who ask about my writing—thank you. Such a simple gesture fuels me for days. I am so blessed that I cannot possibly list everyone's names.

I AM GRATEFUL for the myriad teachers and librarians who fostered my love of books and writing, especially: Betty Chew, the staff of Ballston Spa Public Library, Pat Hodsoll, Ann Ellis, Dave Smith, the relentless and incomparable Emily Adams, and Norman Moyes.

I HAVE BEEN fortunate enough to be encouraged, critiqued, and prodded by many gifted writers, particularly Vivian Fernandez and Rebecca Rector. Thanks also to my supportive online family of writers. I never feel alone.

THANK YOU TO the SCBWI and its talented regional advisors for creating a community that taught me how to be a professional. My SCBWI colleagues show me anything is possible, so long as you keep going.

FINALLY, THANK YOU to Elana Roth, Regina Griffin, and the talented Egmont USA team. You believed in me, taught me, and elevated this book to reality.